The Secrets of Foxglove Lodge

A Blackbird Cabin Mystery
by D. L. Tank

The Secrets of Foxglove Lodge
A Blackbird Cabin Mystery by D. L. Tank

ISBN (print): 979-8-9867305-6-1
ISBN (ebook): 979-8-9867305-5-4

"Tunnel of Love" by Rudy & the Rockets 2025 © David L. Tank

Blackbird Cabin Mystery series
Book 1: The Secret of Blackbird Cabin
Book 2: The Secrets of Foxglove Lodge

"Very few of us are what we seem."
—*Agatha Christie*

Chapter 1

"Didn't you tell me that somewhere in your mysterious past you had participated in a murder mystery dinner?" Megan asked Tony.

"Actually, yes. Quite a few years ago, when I was working at the history center. I helped with the promotion of the event and got drafted into being a seat filler when someone cancelled at the last minute. Why?"

"The Friends of the Library is trying to come up with ideas for a fund raiser, and hosting a murder mystery dinner was one suggestion that seemed especially intriguing. I offered to look into how they're put together."

Megan had recently been invited to join the Northwoods Public Library's Friends group. Even though she and Tony were only part-time residents in the Northwoods, having purchased a small retirement cabin hidden deep in the woods, she regularly used the public library and had gotten to know some of the library staff.

When Tony's debut mystery novel, "The Secret of Blackbird Cabin," was published several months earlier, the library had hosted his book signing event, so both of them had a connection to the library.

"Was the mystery dinner fun?" Megan asked. "How many people were there? Was it difficult to put together?

Would you be willing to write the script for it?"

"Whoa, slow down. As I recall, there were eight people around the table. They needed an exact number so someone could portray each of the suspicious characters. There were also a couple other folks involved; someone doing the serving and a host who was in charge of welcoming the guests and guiding the participants through the story."

"Where'd they hold it?"

"It was a fund raiser for the historical society and they had an old Victorian home, so they held it there. Dinner was in the formal dining room and clues were scattered in various rooms throughout the house. Part of the fun was that participants got to explore the historic home while they were playing the game."

"Sounds complicated."

"Kind of. The biggest problem was that no one involved had organized or even been to a murder mystery dinner before, and every so often the story line kind of ground to a halt while the host made sure that things were moving forward in the right direction. She had to make sure the clues were being discovered in the right order and that the participants were staying in character. Even details like the food being served at the right time were important."

"So," Megan observed, "it sounds like it would have helped if someone involved in organizing it had participated in a murder mystery dinner before."

"Absolutely."

Megan gave Tony her best flirty look.

"If we decide to go ahead with the mystery dinner,

would you, my brilliant and successful mystery writer husband, be willing to write the script?"

"I'm pretty sure you can find a script online. Maybe even for free."

"I know. We checked. But none of the prepackaged scripts look very intriguing. The committee thought it would be more appealing if the mystery had a Northwoods feel to it. Your name came up right away as the perfect person to write the story."

Tony opened his mouth, but before he could utter a word, Megan added, "And I kinda, sorta, already volunteered you."

Chapter 2

Back at their place in the woods, which they'd named Blackbird Cabin, Tony and Megan were busy with a couple of their many projects.

"I'll be in the barn setting up my mushroom farm," Megan said to Tony, who was installing a shower in the cabin's bathroom. "If you need my help, come and get me."

"Okay. Oh, before you go, I need a quick consult."

"About?"

"How important is it to you to have hot water when the sun isn't shining?"

"Odd question."

"I'm not sure if our solar panels will provide enough electricity to run a water heater, so I was thinking about using passive solar to heat it. You know, running the water through black tubing on the roof. But then it occurred to me that we'd only have hot water when the sun is shining."

"Well, up 'til now we've been heating water on the camp stove and washing up in the sink, so anything would be an improvement. What about a gas water heater? Do they sell little ones?"

"I hadn't thought of that. It's worth checking out," he said as Megan headed to the barn. "Good luck with the fungi."

Behind the cabin there was an old barn-like building that had a hidden entrance to a spring house. Long ago it had been used by bootleggers to make and hide their stash. It occurred to Megan that the cool, moist environment might be the perfect space to grow mushrooms.

Early in the spring, Tony had cut some three-foot long maple logs for her and brought them into the barn. She'd ordered some plugs inoculated with mushroom spawn and was now ready to get started.

She began by drilling holes in the sides of the logs. Next she gently hammered the plugs into the holes and sealed them with wax. Then it was a matter of waiting.

When Megan returned from the barn, she checked to see how Tony was doing in the bathroom.

"Wow, you've made good progress on the shower," she said. "I hadn't expected to see it all put together so soon."

"Me either. It was easier to put together than I expected. All I need to do is connect the water."

"Did you figure out how to get hot water?"

"I like your idea of a small gas water heater," he said. "I'll need to check online to see what's available. Would you like to go to the library with me while I use their wifi?"

"How about we do that tomorrow? The Friends group is meeting in the morning to work out the details for the murder mystery fund raiser. Come to think of it, you might want to sit in on that, since you're writing the script. You are writing the script, right?"

"So far I'm still writing it in my head. But I'm making progress. I was able to get a sample script to see just how they're structured and I'm looking forward to putting it together. Should be fun. Do you have a location for it yet that will fit the Northwoods theme?"

"That's something we'll be discussing tomorrow. One of the library's most faithful patrons has a century-old resort that he might be willing to let us use. He's a big fan of murder mysteries — has read every Agatha Christie novel the library has on the shelves — and is intrigued by the idea of using his place for a murder mystery dinner. You should come and talk with him. It might give you some ideas for your story line."

"That's a good idea. But I won't be able to share any details about the murder that I'm planning. One thing that's absolutely clear in all of the research I've done about murder mystery dinners is that no one, not even the host, is supposed to know the details of the murder. When all is revealed at the end, everyone is supposed to be surprised."

"Hopefully that doesn't include you."

Chapter 3

The next day, at the library, Tony scrolled through various sites reviewing different types of water heaters. He was thrilled to discover that small, gas water heaters were readily available, thanks to the popularity of RVs and tiny homes. He selected one that was described as "perfect for off-grid living." It even included a built-in water pump and a shower head. Unfortunately, none of the stores in town had the model he wanted in stock, but he was able to buy it online and have it shipped to the store.

Just as he submitted the order, Megan stepped up behind him.

"Looks like you found what you were looking for," she said, noticing the 'order received' page on the screen.

"I did. Thank you for the suggestion. How are things going with the Friends meeting?"

"Moving ahead nicely. We're ready to talk about the mystery dinner now, so it's time for you to join us."

Megan led the way to the meeting room on the lower level.

"This is really hidden," said Tony, as they reached a door at the end of the nondescript hallway. "I didn't even know this room was down here."

"That's one of the reasons the library is planning to expand. They're sorely in need of a community meeting room."

As they stepped into the cramped meeting space, Megan proudly announced: "This is Tony, my mystery writer husband who has graciously agreed to help us with the script for our murder mystery dinner."

The other members of the committee introduced themselves.

"And this is Rudy Rogers," said Megan, motioning toward a thin, elderly gentleman with styled gray hair. Tony imagined that this is what James Dean would have looked like today if he hadn't died at such a young age.

"Rudy has generously offered the use of his home, Foxglove Lodge, for our murder mystery dinner. He has also agreed to be the face of our new endowment campaign."

"Nice to meet you," said Tony, shaking Rudy's outstretched hand. "I'd love to have a tour of your resort. It's always helpful to experience the environment that I'm writing about."

"I'm right there with you on that," smiled Rudy, leaning back in his chair. "Some of my best songs were inspired by the environment I was in when I wrote them."

"Rudy had a band back in the fifties," explained Megan.

"Really," said Tony. "What were you called?"

"Rudy and the Rockets. We were only together for a few years, but we had some success."

"He's being modest," said Megan. "Rudy wrote 'Blast Off' and "Outta Space."

"I remember those songs," said Tony. "Weren't they in the 'Rock Around the Frat' movie sound track?"

"Wow, you've got quite a memory," said Rudy. "Not many people saw that film. It was actually pretty bad, but the music was good. Of course, I'm a bit biased."

"Those songs were great," said Tony, a bit star struck. "My friends and I had a little garage band back in the '60s and we learned the instrumental 'Blast Off.' That's a great little tune."

"Fortunately," said Rudy, "a couple of those old tunes have recently been resurrected. 'Blast Off' is being used in the sound track of a series of auto commercials..."

"I thought that sounded familiar," said Tony.

"... and 'Outta Space' has resurfaced behind the credits for several popular movies and most recently in an online dance challenge. Suddenly I'm getting royalties on tunes that I wrote when I was a teenager. That sealed the deal for my being able to support the endowment campaign for the library."

"We're calling it the 'We're Outta Space' campaign," Megan pointed out. It'll feature Rudy as the campaign spokesperson.

"That sounds great," said Tony. "I'm looking forward to exploring Foxglove Lodge. Tell me when you're free and I'll be there."

Two days later Tony headed out to Foxglove Lodge, which was only about fifteen minutes from their cabin. The directions he'd been given were to take the county road until he saw a sign for the Foxglove Golf Course, then follow that road past the golf course until he came to two stone pillars marking the entrance to Foxglove Resort.

The pillars were barely visible, nearly hidden by brush and vines after years of neglect. *This must have been a dramatic and welcoming entrance back in the day,* Tony thought. *I wonder what happened to it.*

About a quarter mile from the pillars he came to Foxglove Lodge, which sat along the shore of a medium sized lake. He noticed several smaller cabins flanking the lodge, but it was hard to tell if they were being used.

In fact, it was hard to tell if the lodge itself was being used. It was a magnificent, two-story, log structure that must have been impressive in its heyday, but now appeared unloved and forgotten.

Before Tony could get out of the car, Rudy appeared on the expansive front porch. Aided by an intricately carved cane, he stepped off the porch and made his way to greet his guest.

"Thanks for coming," said Rudy. "I don't get a lot of visitors. It's nice to have someone interested in the old lodge again. About the only people I see here are the owners of the golf course, who wish I'd sell them the place so they could cut down the trees and expand to eighteen holes and level the lodge to put up condominiums."

"Ouch," said Tony, scanning the still beautiful surroundings. "That'd be a shame. Wouldn't it be better to renovate the resort than tear it down?"

"When I bought the place twenty years ago, that's what I had in mind. As you can see, that didn't happen. The first year I was here, I nearly died of a broken heart."

Tony's puzzled look was just the reaction that Rudy had hoped for.

"Not the kind of broken heart I could write a song about," he laughed, "but the kind of broken heart that put me in the hospital for a week, slowed down my physical activities and left me on regular medication."

"Sorry to hear that."

"No, it's okay. Instead of working my tail off renovating the place, I've enjoyed the resort as my own personal sanctuary, where I can sit back, reflect and appreciate whatever years I still have on this earth."

He scanned the foxglove covered shoreline.

"Enough of this maudlin talk. Would you like a tour?"

Chapter 4

"Let me get my camera," Tony said, scurrying back to his car. "I've been asked to shoot some pictures for a brochure encouraging legacy gifts for the library. The committee is pretty flattered that you've agreed to be the face of their campaign."

"I'm flattered to have been asked. It's been a long, long time since I've done anything in the public eye, and I'm realizing that I kinda missed it."

"Have you been working behind the scenes in the music business?"

"Not even close. After my days as a musician, I took a job at a local cooperative health clinic. Back then, co-ops looked like the direction medical care would be taking. My job was logging in patient records and, yes, it was as tedious and boring as it sounds. I started exploring ways to streamline the record-keeping process."

"It's easy to forget that computers weren't a thing back then."

"No kidding. When I started, everything was paper files."

Rudy continued telling his story as he led Tony up onto the porch,

"About that time, I got married and thought about starting a family. Turned out, that wasn't meant to be. My wife began having a variety of health problems that no one at my clinic seemed able to diagnose. So we visited a number of other clinics. Each time we saw a new doctor, we'd have to bring along printed copies of her medical records. I'm not sure if the new doctors even looked at the other doctors' records."

Rudy took a deep breath, leaned on his cane, then sat down on the nearest of several wicker chairs that were lined up on the porch. Tony followed his lead and propped his butt on the porch railing.

"At one point," Rudy continued, "she was prescribed a drug that was not supposed to be used in conjunction with a medication that had been prescribed by a different doctor at a different clinic."

"What happened?"

"We caught it—through our own research—but by the time we did, it had set her back."

"And your wife?"

"She passed away two years later. They never did agree on what caused her death."

"I'm sorry."

"Thanks. At that point, I independently devoted all of my energies into creating a computer program that would allow a patient's records to quickly and easily be shared between doctors; even between different health systems, as long as they all used the software that I developed. It was hugely successful.

"Eventually, I sold the program to a national healthcare company so it could be implemented more broadly.

Seemed like a good idea at the time, and it set me up financially for retirement."

"Is that when you bought this place?"

"Yup. That's when I decided to shift gears and go into the resort business. As I mentioned earlier, that plan didn't last long, thanks to my broken heart. And here we are today."

Rudy used his cane to help him stand up.

"Let me give you a tour of the lodge."

As he looked through the front door, Tony felt as if he was stepping into the set of a Hallmark holiday movie. The well-worn plank floors squeaked a greeting as he set foot inside. Massive, varnished log beams spanned the entire room. Straight ahead in the center of the massive room there was a beautiful staircase with natural log railings. A huge, fieldstone fireplace was front and center on one wall, flanked on both sides by log-framed windows that looked into the woods. A gigantic moose head looked down from the wall above the six-inch thick, rustic, wooden mantel.

"I didn't realize there were moose up here," Tony said. "Are you a hunter?"

"No," Rudy laughed. "Bullwinkel came with the place. There's a whole room filled with trophies hidden back behind the dining room. Nearly everything in here is original to when it was a thriving resort. My goal was to keep it as authentic as possible. At least I lived up to that part of my plan."

Off to one side of the hearth room was a game room, with a ping-pong table, pool table and a table-height electronic bowling alley from the 1950s. A dining room with seating for sixteen people was on the opposite side of the great hall. A wall of windows provided diners with a lovely view of the lake. The kitchen, while having been updated with modern appliances, still had the feel of being untouched by the twenty-first century.

"That's my room back there," Rudy said, motioning toward a closed door just down the hallway, across from the kitchen. "I don't need much space. And it's got the nicest view of the lake. I believe it was the owners' suite when the resort was in full swing. It's handy for greeting guests, but hidden far enough back to feel private."

They made their way up the wooden staircase. The second floor guest rooms were small, but comfortable. A single, large bathroom served them all.

"Adding en suite bathrooms was a necessity if I was going to reopen this place," Rudy explained, "but I never got beyond the design phase. Maybe that's just as well. The place would have lost it's historical charm if I'd have made all of the changes expected by today's lodgers."

"Thank you for the tour," said Tony as they stepped back onto the porch. "I'm sure the murder mystery participants will be enthralled by the resort. I'll bet that the local history buffs would love to tour this place, too."

"That's what I've thought. I'm planning to will the resort to the local historical society. I can imagine it being run as a living history site to show people what it was like in the Northwoods when resorts were king."

"That's fantastic! Are they excited to learn of your plans?"

"I've only told the society president and asked that he keep it under wraps for now. I'm planning to stick around for awhile yet," he laughed, "and I don't want the society members to get antsy for me to croak."

"I don't think you'll need to worry about that."

"I'm also leaving a considerable amount to the library for their building project. The Friends group president has taken a real interest in helping me with that. She and I have had some interesting conversations. I'm also leaving a sizable gift to the homeless shelter.

"When I'm gone and everything is divided up according to my wishes, I want my net worth to be zero. I came into the world with nothing, and that's the way I want to go out."

"That's a great attitude. Mind if I ask a question?"

"Go for it."

"Megan and I want to draft our wills, but aren't sure if we need a lawyer to witness it."

"All you need are the signatures of two witnesses. They can be anyone who isn't included as a beneficiary. I asked the young couple staying in my cabin to witness mine."

"Thanks. Well, I suppose I'd better take some pictures of you for the brochure. Any suggestions on where we should shoot them?"

"You haven't seen all of the resort, yet. Keep your eyes out for a picturesque spot as I show you the rest of the grounds."

Chapter 5

"How big is this place?" Tony asked as they left the lodge.

"Originally, it was two forties. About half of that was the golf course."

"The golf course was part of the resort?"

"Right. There was also a tennis court by the clubhouse and two shuffleboard courts here in front of the lodge, near that concrete bench over there. Only the finest for Foxglove's guests."

Rudy led the way to the lake. Between the lodge and the shore, hundreds of tall plants were just beginning to bloom.

"That'd be a beautiful spot to take your picture," said Tony. "What kind of flowers are those?"

"Foxglove. Namesake of the lodge. They were planted a century ago, when the resort first opened."

"Amazing that they're still alive," Tony said as he scoped out the best spots for his photos.

"These are the great, great, great grand babies of the originals," Rudy explained as Tony began snapping pictures. "Foxgloves are biennials; they bloom only in their second year, then die. But they're prolific reseeders, keeping the strain growing long after they're gone."

"Seriously? I don't think we could find a more fitting background for a brochure about leaving a legacy. Step a few feet to your left," Tony instructed as he snapped away. "Perfect. Now try leaning on your cane and looking directly into the camera. Imagine that you're telling the readers how important it is to include the library in their wills."

He shot several more pictures among the blooms; some with the lodge in the background, others with Rudy pensively facing the lake.

"I can't wait to show Megan these pictures," he said. "She loves gardening, but it seems like the critters nip off everything she tries to grow."

"Then foxglove would be perfect for her to plant. They're toxic, so the deer and rabbits won't touch them. You might have noticed the area with the high fence near the back door. That's to keep the deer out of my herb and vegetable garden."

"Do you grow a lot of your own food?"

"Lately, I've been experimenting with different kinds of greens. I've got some berry bushes, too, on the other side of the lodge. There's no better way to start the day than with a spinach, kale and raspberry smoothie."

Tony gave a bit of a grimace.

Rudy tapped his chest. "It's supposed to be good for the ol' ticker. You should try it. Tastes best with home-grown produce."

"I'll leave the gardening to Megan," said Tony. "More work than I'm willing to commit to. Do you do all of this alone?"

"I tried to, but with my heart issues, it's been a bit too much. I've recently gotten some help.

"You might have noticed these cottages when you drove in," Rudy continued as they followed the walking path. "At one time, there were six of them, but only three are still standing."

"Are they being used?"

"Just one. This spring, a young couple showed up at my door and asked if I rented out the cabins. I told them that I originally had intended to, but wasn't able to keep them up, so no, they weren't for rent.

"They explained that they'd just arrived in the area looking for work and were desperate for a place to stay. We talked for a while—seemed like nice folks—and we came to an agreement that they could stay here in Bluebird Cottage."

He nodded as they passed one of the three cabins; the only one that had curtains in the windows and flowers in the window boxes.

"We agreed they could stay until they got on their feet, in exchange for their fixing up the cabin and helping me with the yard and gardens. Their timing was perfect."

"Sounds like it's working out for both of you."

"Yes, and I appreciate having them nearby. The young woman stops in every couple of days to check on me."

The path along the lakeshore took a bend and began to rise.

"The resort sits on a peninsula," Rudy explained. "We have lake frontage on three sides. It's an exceptional piece of property."

"What's that?" Tony asked, as they came to a huge

structure extending over the water.

"That's the reason I bought this place. The lower level is a boathouse. You can dock six boats in there, out of the elements."

"Is your boat in there?"

"I may live 'on the lake,'" he laughed, lifting his cane as he made air quotes, "but I'm a landlubber. Everyone expects I should have a big ol' pontoon boat, but being on the water has never been my thing. I don't even fish. Water sports had nothing to do with my buying this place."

"Is that another cottage above the boathouse?" Tony asked, noticing the windows flanking the side of the second floor. "They'd have quite a view."

Rudy stopped, put both hands on the top of his cane and looked affectionately at the old structure.

"The upstairs was a dance hall. Sixty-five years ago, I played here with Rudy and the Rockets. One of my favorite songs was inspired by this place."

He paused, remembering his youth.

"Let me show it to you."

They made their way past a stairway that led down to the lake.

"Should we go down?" Tony asked.

"A boathouse is a boathouse. You've seen one, you've seen them all."

He instead led Tony to a set of three somewhat rickety steps that led to the upper level of the boathouse. Retrieving a key from behind a placque depicting the sun and moon, he unlocked the door.

"Welcome to the Starlight Ballroom," Rudy said with a flourish. "This is the reason I bought Foxglove Resort."

The room was much larger than Tony had expected. He was surprised to see that it was still recognizable as a dance hall. Immediately to the left was the stage, raised about two feet above the dance floor. Maroon velvet curtains still covered the back wall.

There were two skylights positioned above the stage. The rest of the ceiling was painted a dark blue and filled with silver stars, some forming recognizable constellations, others randomly spread out to fill the seemingly vast space. Small tables, each with four chairs, were placed beneath the windows, looking as if they were waiting for the crowd to show up for the next dance.

At the far end of the room were glass doors leading out to a balcony overlooking the water.

"Most boathouses did not have such a fabulous room above them," explained Rudy. "Listen to this."

He stepped onto the stage and began tapping out a rhythm with his cane. Then he began singing the chorus to an old Buddy Holly tune.

"The acoustics in here are fantastic," he said. "You barely need amplification, which was a good thing back in the day when we didn't have much to work with."

"When did you play here?" Tony asked.

"Summer of '62. A couple of years after Buddy's plane went down. We covered several of his songs. Had to because of requests. But we also played our own original tunes. One of them, 'Tunnel of Love,' was inspired by this place."

Tony gave no sign of recognition.

"Don't feel bad if you haven't heard of it. It was the B-side of 'Blast Off.' Even though it never got any radio play, it's the song that meant the most to me."

"Why's that?"

"I'll show you."

He led Tony across the stage and pulled aside the thick curtain at the back, exposing a storage area with a hidden doorway. He opened the door to reveal a stairway.

"Follow me."

He flipped a very old switch and a single bare bulb illuminated the stairs. At the bottom, to the right, was a partially open door. Tony could see the sun reflecting off the water inside the boat house. Also at the bottom of the stairs, to the left, was another door. Rudy put his hand on the latch, paused dramatically, then pulled it open.

"Welcome to the Tunnel of Love," he smiled. "The night we played here, I followed this tunnel up to the lodge— it comes out in a little nook behind the kitchen—and I had a bit of a fling with the cutest little housekeeper I've ever laid eyes on. Definitely a night to remember. The next day I wrote 'Tunnel of Love.'"

The two of them took the path back to the lodge rather than using the tunnel, which was filled with spider webs and obviously hadn't been used in some time.

"I've got something I'd still like to show you," Rudy said, leading the way back inside the lodge and down the hall to his personal living space. "This area is off limits to the dinner guests, but, if I remember correctly, you mentioned that you were in a garage band in your younger days."

"Yes, I did."

"Then you'll get a kick out of this," he said as he opened the door to his room. Unlike the rest of the lodge, which faithfully maintained its century-old ambience, this suite appeared to have been spirited in from the 1950s and '60s. Framed concert posters adorned the walls: Dion and the Bellmonts, Chuck Berry, Steppenwolf. A tie-dyed spread covered the bed. Several guitars were proudly displayed in one corner.

"Nice collection," Tony said, admiring the vintage instruments.

"Those are the ones I'm willing to keep out." He pulled aside a huge Woodstock flag that was covering one wall to reveal a hidden closet filled with speakers, mic stands and instrument cases.

"This is my pride and joy," Rudy said, pulling out a rectangular, tweed-covered guitar case. He carefully laid it on the floor, opened the lid and gently lifted out a beautiful electric guitar with a two-tone sunburst finish. "It's the guitar I played when I wrote most of my songs."

"Is that what I think it is?"

"Yes sir—a '57 Fender Strat. The love of my life."

"I thought the girl from 'Tunnel of Love' was the love of your life."

Rudy laughed. "I guess that night we were a threesome."

He handed the guitar to Tony. "Give it a try."

"This is in mint condition," Tony said, fingering a few chords. "It's beautiful."

"Found it at a pawn shop back in '61, can you believe that? "

Tony noticed several papers and a photo lying in the bottom of the case.

"Is that you?" He pointed to a black and white, autographed publicity photo of Rudy and the Rockets. A much younger Rudy was hugging the very same guitar.

"Pretty spiffy looking, weren't we," he said, handing the picture to Tony. "That picture was taken the day I bought this guitar. Our fan club sent them out. The president of the club and a couple of her friends spent an entire afternoon forging our signatures. My actual handwriting is not nearly this good."

Tony held up the picture to compare the *then* image with the *now* scene before him, then set it on a nearby shelf.

"What other memories have you got in there?"

Rudy flipped through the other papers.

"I've got a couple of set lists from when we were at our prime. And my original handwritten lyrics to 'Tunnel of Love' and "Outta Space.'"

"What wonderful memories to have hung on to."

"Yes. They're irreplaceable."

He laughed, holding up the corner of a file folder.

"I've got my will and real estate papers in here, too. I figured that if the lodge catches on fire, the first thing I'm going to save is this guitar, so I might as well keep all the important stuff together."

"Thanks for letting me play this," Tony said, strumming a few more chords. "I am honored."

"It needs to be played more often," Rudy said. "I think I'll leave it out for a while to remind me."

Steadying himself with his cane and suddenly looking very old, Rudy closed the nearly empty case, concealing the old set lists and other papers, and put it back in the closet.

"I've taken really good care of this guitar over the years," he said, taking the guitar back from Tony and placing it on a stand. "Too bad *I* haven't held up as well as it has."

Chapter 6

"How are ticket sales going?," Tony asked Megan. "Do we have our eight dinner guests?"

"As of yesterday, we have seven confirmed. Three men and four women. We've had a couple more inquiries, so I don't think we'll have a problem filling the last spot."

"Give me a list when you do, so I can finish creating the characters. But don't tell me anything about the participants beyond their age and gender. I don't want their real identities to influence me when I'm deciding who committed the murder."

"I'm not the one selling the tickets, so I don't know who they are, either," said Megan. "I'm glad that you're taking this seriously."

"Wouldn't you?"

"Good point."

"The thing I miss most about this writing project," confessed Tony, "is not getting to bounce more of my ideas off you."

"And I miss not getting an inside track on who dunnit."

"You'll find out soon enough... along with everyone else. Will Rudy be the host?"

"We'd hoped so, but he declined. He said he'd rather

not be home during the dinner; that it might feel odd having strangers snooping around the place."

"He's not changing his mind about letting us use the lodge, is he?"

"No. He's still okay with our using the place. He'd just like to not be involved. Will that change your story line?"

"I'm going with a '60s rock 'n' roll theme and thought it'd be fun to have him be part of it. Maybe even get him to play his guitar. Did anyone else offer to be the host?"

"The committee kinda drafted me. Unless you'll do it? Your name came up, but I didn't think I should agree on your behalf."

"Like you did for me writing the script?"

Megan just grinned.

"I can see you as the host," Tony said, "all dolled up in your love beads and peasant dress welcoming the guests. But weren't you overseeing the food?"

"I was, so I was already planning to be there."

"Who'll do the food?"

"We're farming that out to the committee. Several people will be responsible for preparing the different courses and bringing them to the lodge, kind of like a potluck dinner. Martha Hopkins, president of the Friends group, agreed to take on the serving duties. She said she's got a cute little maid's outfit she can wear."

Tony recalled meeting Martha when he'd met with the Friends group and managed to resist making a comment.

Martha continued: "I'm hoping to have some fresh mushrooms by then to include on the dinner salads. Rudy said we're welcome to pick fresh greens from his gardens there at the lodge."

"For what seems like a small event, there sure are a lot of parts and pieces to pull together."

"Not the least of which is your script. How's that coming along?"

"I'm making progress. I've got the location. And the theme. And most of the characters. The only things I still need to figure out are who gets killed, who did it and why."

"That's all? I'd better leave you to your writing. We'll be sending out the tickets in a few days with the character assignments. The dinner is two weeks after that."

"Don't worry, I'll get it done. I work well with a deadline."

She flashed him the peace sign.

Two days later, Tony handed Megan eight sheets of paper.

"I wrote out the name and basic traits for each character. All you have to do is include the appropriate sheet with each confirmation letter."

"Interesting names," said Megan, thumbing through the papers. "Sony Bunyan, Cher Bunyan, Elvis Presquisle. You do know it's pronounced Presk Aisle, right?"

"Yes, but it kinda looks like Preskley."

Megan continued reviewing the names: Byrdie Finch, Buddy Hollyhock, Janis Choplin.

"I am definitely detecting an attempt to mash up classic rock with the Northwoods."

"I wanted the names to be fun and memorable. And nothing too likely to be confused with the real person who might be playing the game. Which wasn't too hard since I don't know their true identities."

"I love these last two names: Chuck Cranberry and Mama Bass. Quite the cast of characters."

"Thank you."

"I'll bring these sheets along this afternoon when the committee meets," she said. "Does the registrar have to assign these to specific guests?"

"I created the characters based on the same general age and gender of the anonymous list of participants you gave me, but if it doesn't match perfectly, that's fine. It might be more fun if a 60-year-old man is cast as a 25-year-old woman."

"Very Monty Pythonesque. I'm assuming you have back-up copies."

"Absolutely. I'll be working with them as I put together a more detailed packet of information for each participant. They'll get that information when they arrive."

"Will I get a copy of the script as host? I'm a little nervous that I might screw things up."

"Before the guests arrive, I'll give you an instruction booklet you can follow to guide everyone through the dinner, course by course. It's best that you don't know the details of the mystery, though. That way you can't inadvertently sway the players one way or another in their solving the mystery. Think of yourself as the person graciously welcoming guests to 'your' lodge and making sure everyone is enjoying themselves."

"Will I get a character name as host?"

"How about Megan Moonflower?"

"Love it. You'll be there, right?"

"I'll be lurking in the shadows to monitor how things

are progressing. If the group starts to veer off the rails, I'll help get everyone back on track."

"Want to be my co-host?"

"Let's play it by ear. We can at least welcome the guests together. That'll keep folks from wondering who that guy is who's hanging around eavesdropping and snapping pictures."

Chapter 7

"Do you want to ride over to the lodge with me this morning?" Tony asked his wife.

"I wasn't planning to get there until about four, when everyone's supposed to drop off their food for the dinner. Martha offered to swing by and pick me up on her way to the lodge. She's interested in seeing my mushroom garden and offered to help me with my first harvest. Why are you going so early?"

"Rudy would like to meet me there to give me a more complete tour of the building and help me decide the best spots to hide the clues. Once we're done with that, he's planning to disappear for the rest of the day. I figured I'd just hang around and enjoy the scenery. Maybe take a nap."

"Sounds like a plan. Don't forget to take along some snacks."

Rudy was sitting on the front porch when Tony pulled up to the lodge.

"Are you all set for your big day?" he said as Tony, carrying a leather satchel, exited the vehicle.

"As set as I'll be, I guess. How about you?"

"You've got the tough job," Rudy replied. "All I'm doing is providing the venue."

"Don't underestimate the scene of the crime."

"Oh, I'm not. I'm quite the mystery buff. I've read every one of Agatha Christie's mysteries, including the plays and short stories, and the settings always have an important roll. I'm curious to see what part Foxglove Lodge will play in the mystery you've written."

Tony made the motion of zipping shut his lips.

"Fine. But I bet I can figure out the mystery when I see the clues you're hiding."

"Maybe, but I'm not going to tell you if you're correct."

As they walked through the house, Tony studied each room, looked at his notes, then reached into his satchel and left something of significance that could be found by the dinner guests. Once in a while, Rudy would suggest a slightly different location to make finding the clue a bit more of a challenge.

After they were finished in the lodge, they spent some time placing a few more clues in the yard and gardens. When Tony's satchel was empty, they returned to the lodge.

"Good luck with your dinner," Rudy said. "Be sure to lock up when you leave."

•　•　•　•　•

"Everything set?" Megan asked Tony as she and Martha arrived at the lodge.

"As set as I can make it. I'm keeping my fingers crossed

that the clues will be found and make sense."

"This is such a beautiful place," Martha said looking around and taking a deep breath. "Makes me feel young again."

"Yes, it is idyllic," said Megan. "Tony's told me all about it."

"Let me show you to the kitchen," Tony said.

"No need," said Martha. "I know where it is."

"I didn't realize you'd been here before," said Megan.

"Oh. These old lodges are all the same," said Martha, who was about the same age as Megan. "When I was young, I spent many a summer working at the resorts up here. Each of them had a great room in the front, a dining room overlooking the lake, and a kitchen behind the stairs."

"Tony," Megan said, "how about you give us a hand carrying things in from the car."

Besides some of the food, she and Martha had brought along place settings for eight as well as serving plates, trays and utensils.

"We didn't want to assume we could use the dishes that were here," Megan said as Tony carried the last box into the kitchen.

"Look at this," said Martha, peeking into one of the cabinets. "He's still got some of those old Red Wing serving bowls. Do you think he'd mind if we used them? I love the way they hold the heat on the serving table."

Another car pulled up to the lodge. It was the three other members of the Friends group who were delivering their contributions to the evening meal.

After they brought their food into the kitchen, Tony

gave the whole group a quick tour of the lodge, being careful to not direct anyone's attention to the clues he'd placed earlier.

"Can we go up there?" Megan asked, noticing a small stairway in a nook at the very back of the lodge, just down the hall from the kitchen.

"I'm not sure where that leads," said Tony. "Rudy didn't take me up there."

"That's probably where the help had their rooms," Martha interjected. "At least, that's what I'm guessing."

"Could be," said Tony. "But I'm not comfortable taking you into places that Rudy didn't show me."

After the other women had left, Megan said to Martha, "Let's start organizing the dinner by courses. My notes for the murder mystery have the meal divided into four courses—appetizers, salad, entree and dessert—each served about half an hour apart."

"When do they solve the mystery?" asked Martha.

"There's time allotted for discussion and discovery of clues during and between each of the courses," she said. "My job, as host, will be to announce when it's time to reveal the next set of clues, coinciding with each course. At the end of the meal, the guests will all meet together in the great room for coffee or tea, where they can each reveal who they think did it and how it was done."

"What if no one gets it right?"

"Then I didn't do a very good job of writing the script," Tony laughed as he stepped into the kitchen. "Don't worry, by the end of the night, all will be revealed."

Chapter 8

The guests began arriving right at six. First to drive up was a woman dressed in a flowing, oversized, flowered dress with a ring of daisies in her hair. Megan guessed that she was in her early forties. Hanging from each ear was an earring in the shape of a fish on a stringer.

"Welcome to Foxglove Lodge," said Megan. "I'm guessing from your outfit that you're Mama Bass."

The woman flashed a huge smile. "Oh, I'm so glad I got it right. I had the hardest time trying to figure out what to wear. Should I emphasize the Mama part or the Bass part? My first thought was to dress as Lance Bass's mother—he is quite the mama's boy, you know—but I had no idea what his mama dressed like. Then it dawned on me, duh, that his group, NYSNC, wasn't even around until the '90s, and that didn't fit with the flower child theme at all, so 'Bye, Bye, Bye' to Lance Bass. Fortunately, as I was looking through some old LPs at the thrift store, I came across an album by Mama Cass— her song 'Dream a Little Dream of Me' is fantastic, by the way—and I found this Mama dress right there at the thrift store, but, oh, what to do about Bass? Then, the next day, I discovered these silly fish earrings at a tourist shop—not sure if they're bass, maybe they're perch—but here I am, Mama Bass at your service."

"Nice to meet you, Mama Bass," Megan said, realizing that since she hadn't been involved with the ticketing, she had no idea of her talkative guest's real-life identity. "Please have a seat on the porch."

Megan was so busy listening to Mama that she didn't hear a car drive in when Byrdie Finch arrived. Byrdie had short blond hair and appeared to be in her early thirties. She was wearing hiking boots, cargo shorts and a tie-dyed T-shirt that said "Bird Nerd." The shirt looked brand new. Around her neck hung a small pair of toy binoculars.

Megan asked Byrdie to join Mama Cass on the porch, where she pretended to peer through her binoculars to see what birds she could discover in the woods surrounding the lodge, while Mama went on and on about the time she'd once seen a parakeet in a tree that must have escaped from someone's house and wondered if Byrdie had a parakeet on her life list. She politely said she did. Said she saw it in Antarctica.

A black SUV pulled up next. A couple who appeared to be in their mid fifties stepped out. They were dressed as one would expect Sonny and Cher to look, with the exception of Sonny wearing logging boots and Cher sporting an Up North T-shirt under her faux fur vest.

"Hi, I'm Sonny," the man said, cheerfully holding his hand out to Megan.

The woman strutted up beside Sonny, flicked her long black hair and gave him a disdainful look, then said to Megan, "And I'm his better half. At least for now."

Tony sat inconspicuously on the nearby concrete bench, watching and listening as the visitors arrived.

This is way more interesting than I imagined, he thought, appreciating the effort the guests had made to get into character. *Tonight is either going to be totally awesome or a complete train wreck.*

A Jeep Wrangler with a storm trooper cutout in the rear window pulled up and someone who looked like The King himself jumped out of the car wearing a jumpsuit, guitar in hand.

"So nice to have you join us Elvis," said Megan, getting into the spirit of the event. "Did you have a good flight up from Graceland?"

"Yes, Ma'am. We stopped on the way for a peanut butter and banana sandwich with a side of bacon."

"I see you brought your guitar. Will you be playing something for us tonight?"

"Yes, Ma'am, that would be my honor."

Wow, thought Megan. *This guy's in full-on Elvis mode. Nothing Northwoodsy about him.*

Then he swivelled his hips, hit a chord on his guitar, and belted out: "You ain't nothin' but a Hodag, growlin' all the time!"

Elvis danced his way to the porch.

Next to arrive was Janis Choplin. She had a bottle in one hand and a cigarette in the other.

"Groovy pad you've got here," she said in a voice that sounded more like Betty Boop than the sixties rock star. "Sorry, but Bobby McGee couldn't make it tonight. He's too busy drivin' around the lake in his freakin' pontoon boat. Say's it's all about freedom. But freedom's just another word for nothin' left to lose."

Definitely going to be an interesting evening, thought Tony, catching a glance from Megan.

Buddy Hollyhock, wearing black plastic glasses from Dollar Tree, pulled up in a rusty Dodge Caravan.

"I really need to get this heap fixed before winter," he said as he was greeted by Megan. "I've heard that the Northwoods isn't the best place to drive around with a busted heater."

"Yeah, probably not a good idea," said Megan. "You might want to consider flying."

Ouch! thought Tony, wondering if his wife was aware that the real Buddy Holly and his band had nearly frozen to death in a broken down bus when they played in northern Wisconsin shortly before Buddy died in a plane crash.

From the porch, Elvis belted out "don't be cruel."

Buddy hurried to the porch before Megan could stick her foot any farther down her throat.

Megan checked her watch.

"It's about time to get started," she announced as she stepped onto the porch. "We're still waiting for one of our guests to arrive, but I wanted to welcome you more formally and introduce my ... co-host." She nodded toward Tony, who walked up beside her.

"I am Megan Moonflower and this is..." She hesitated, realizing Tony hadn't given himself a name.

"Moon Dog," he jumped in, making up his moniker on the spot.

Just then, a pick-up truck pulled in and skidded to a stop. Out jumped a thin man, maybe fifty years old, with wavy black hair, wearing a purple sport coat, a white dress shirt, and a bow tie. If it wasn't for his cooler-than-cool swagger, he'd look like a total nerd.

"Sorry I'm late," he said, sauntering toward the lodge. "I never get anywhere early. And I'd like my pay now, before we play."

"You must be Chuck Cranberry," Megan said as the rock icon duck walked his way onto the porch as if he were stepping into the spotlight before an adoring crowd.

Elvis and Buddy both stretched out their arms and bowed down to him.

"So glad that all of you could join us this evening," Megan said once Chuck had found a seat. "One of you has committed murder. The rest of us will follow the clues you left behind and, at the end, expose your crime. Every one of you could have a motive and anyone of you could be a suspect. Even the murderer won't know until the end if they did it."

The participants began eyeing each other suspiciously.

"We'll begin with a few appetizers out here on the porch," Megan said.

Martha, wearing her maid's outfit, brought out a large tray of crackers, sliced venison sausage, cheese curds and strawberries.

"There are beverages here in these coolers," Tony said. "Take what you'd like. And then please explore the grounds while you get to know each other... in character, of course."

Megan added: "In about half an hour, I'll ring the dinner bell signaling that you should return to the lodge. Come into the dining room for the next course, during which you'll receive a secret document with intimate details about your character.

"Until then, enjoy strolling the grounds and keep your eyes peeled for anything that might be a clue to a murder. But watch your back. The person next to you could be the killer!"

Chapter 9

Tony casually strolled the grounds as the participants began exploring the area surrounding Foxglove Lodge. He had his camera with him and shot a number of candid photos.

He was pleased to see that the participants were talking with each other and appeared to be staying in character. Even though Sonny and Cher had arrived together, Cher seemed intent on chatting up Elvis, and Elvis didn't seem to mind.

Sonny, on the other hand, wandered about on his own for a few minutes, then sat down on a stump overlooking the water. He seemed deep in thought when Byrdie stepped up behind him.

"Hi," she said in a quiet voice. "I'm Byrdie. This is a beautiful place, isn't it. Have you been here before?"

"Oh." He paused. "No. My first time. Never been here before. I'm Sonny, by the way."

"Nice to meet you. Do you have any idea how this all works? It's my first murder mystery dinner and I'm not quite sure what to expect. Or, more specifically, what's expected of me."

"All I know is that we, as the characters we were assigned, have to figure out who was the killer. Not quite sure, though, how we go about doing that."

"Seems odd that we don't know who was killed. I hope it's not me. That would kind of take the fun out of the rest of the night. Who do you think got it?" she made the motion of a knife slashing across her neck.

"Not a clue. Do you think someone was killed by getting their throat cut?"

"Oh, no, just being dramatic." She raised her toy binoculars to her eyes. "Have you seen any interesting birds along the lake shore?"

Tony moved on down the path where he noticed Buddy talking with Chuck. They stopped their conversation as soon as they noticed him.

"Don't mind me," said Tony. "I'm just making sure everyone is enjoying themselves."

"We're good," said Chuck.

"Yes," said Buddy. "Simply comparing our favorite gauge of guitar strings."

"And what did you discover?"

"We both play rock 'n' roll, but we play very differently," explained Chuck. "I want a string that bends easily and slides across the neck."

"And I prefer a heavier gauge," said Buddy. "I need strings that can handle my powerful down strokes without breaking. How about you? Do you play?"

"A little," said Tony. "I'm good with whatever strings the music store has on sale."

Tony noticed a couple of people talking farther down the trail, near the cabins, so he excused himself and headed their direction, snapping a few pictures as he walked.

By the time he got there, however, they had disappeared.

It occurred to him that he'd better head back to the lodge and see how Megan and Martha were doing with preparations for the first dinner course in the dining room. The menu for that course was simple; a tossed salad and fresh bread. The important part of it wasn't the food so much as that each guest would receive more details about his or her character. That and the big reveal of who was killed.

•　•　•　•　•

As soon as they heard the dinner bell, the squadron of er satz flower children returned to the lodge. Some came alone, others in groups of two or three.

"Please come in and find your spot," Megan instructed the guests. "Each place has an envelope with your name on it."

The long, wooden table had eight chairs; four along each side. At the head of the table, farthest from the door, was a chair with a framed portrait propped on it, as if it was another guest in absentia. The man in the portrait had curly black hair, neatly trimmed to just below the top of his ears. Sitting on the tip of his nose was a pair of granny glasses, which he was looking over, not through. He was wearing a black turtleneck under a light blue Nehru jacket with an upturned collar. Around his neck, hanging from a string of love beads, was a multi-colored peace symbol medallion.

"What's the deal with the picture?" asked Cher, nodding toward the portrait. "I mean, it's a nice enough picture, not a bad looking guy, but who is he and why's he crashing our little soiree?"

"Glad you asked," answered Megan. "The gentleman in the picture is named Weasel Leech. He is one of the most powerful—and many would say corrupt—record company executives in the world. He has grown rich off the talents of numerous musicians and artists through trickery, deceit, legal loopholes and by just plain being a horrible person. Each of you will discover, when reading the information in your envelope, how you, personally, have had a relationship with him.

"That doesn't narrow it down much," joked Mama Bass. "Couldn't you find someone I haven't had a relationship with?"

Her comment got a good laugh around the table.

"We requested that Weasel join us this evening," Megan continued, "however he did not respond to our invitation. As best as we can discover, he has not been seen for nearly a week. The big question: What happened to him?" She let the question dramatically hang in the air for a few seconds.

"No.

"One.

"Knows."

A soft chorus of oohhs floated across the table.

This is great, thought Tony, proud of the job Megan was doing as host. *They're really getting into the spirit of the game.*

"No one, that is, except for the person or persons responsible for his disappearance. Someone in this room knows what happened to Weasel Leech! It's up to you to figure out who."

The guests looked around at each other, studying their faces, as Martha brought out the salads.

"Enjoy your first course," Martha announced as she placed before each person a tasty-looking bowl of mixed greens, mushrooms, cherry tomatoes and slivered carrots, topped with raspberries. "Everything is locally grown and was harvested today. I'll be back in a second with some fresh bread."

She soon returned with two baskets of sliced marble rye, still warm from the oven.

"There's butter, comb honey and strawberry jam on the table for you to pass and share. Enjoy."

"Thank you, Martha," Megan said. "Now is the time for each of you to open your envelope. It includes private information about your personal connection to Weasel Leech."

The guests opened their envelopes and carefully read what was inside. At the top of the page were the words:

FOR YOUR EYES ONLY

This was followed by details about the person's interactions with the music mogul and how his actions affected that person's career and life. The note continued:

Others will try to discover your secret. You may, but do not need to, volunteer this information. If someone specifically asks you about it, you can try to be deceptive with your answer, but you may not lie. By the end of this dinner course, you must have revealed your secret Weasel Leech connection to at least one other dinner guest.

Also in the envelope was a slip of paper with a specific

location in the lodge, with the following instructions:

Sometime during this dinner course, discreetly go to the location listed here and look for a clue as to what happened to Mr. Leech. When you return to the table, please share this information with others as you feel appropriate. You must tell at least one person what you found before we move on to the next course. Happy hunting.

Also included was a smaller envelope that said *Do Not Open Until the Next Course.*

Megan walked to the head of the table and rested her hands on the portrait of the missing music mogul.

"Weasel, Weasel, Weasel," she slowly and deliberately said to the image, "what have you done?"

She scanned the faces of those at the table, then grinned.

"You all look just a little bit guilty. Enjoy your meal."

Chapter 10

The information about Weasel Leech did not sit well with the individual dinner guests. As they munched on their salad and bread, they couldn't keep what they'd learned to themselves. Almost immediately they began complaining about how Weasel had treated them.

"Can you believe this guy?" Mama said to those around her. "That so and so kept my royalties; said he was hanging onto them for safe keeping. Safe keeping for who? Not for Mama Bass, that's for sure. He used my royalties for booze and drugs and gambling! Hey, Mr. Weasel, Mama could have enjoyed some of that money!"

"If he gave you the money," Janis interjected, "you'd have probably just spent it on booze and drugs yourself."

"Exactly! He stole my booze and drug money. What'd he do to you?"

"Maybe you were lucky," said Janis, flapping her info sheet in the air. "According to this, he kept me drunk and stoned so I'd do anything he wanted without me complaining."

Elvis joined the conversation. "It's not so much what he did to me, as what he kept me from doing for myself. Colonel Leech—yes, that's what he made me call him—

wouldn't let me choose the songs I wanted to sing, the movies I wanted to act in or the places I could perform. Some of the stuff he had me singing—especially in those movies—was rubbish."

"I have to agree with you there," chimed in Sonny. "But don't be so hard on yourself. He made you a world-wide sensation."

"World wide!? He never let me perform outside of the United States. There was something shady in his past and he was afraid he'd get arrested if he stepped foot off U.S. soil."

"Why didn't you tour on your own?" asked Byrdie.

"He was always with me. To top that, I was a naive young man and didn't know any better when I signed a contract with him saying he'd get fifty percent of what-ever I made."

"You mean fifteen percent," said Chuck. "That's the standard."

"So I learned. What'd he do to you?"

"I toured all over," said Chuck, "but he'd collect the take at the door and pay me after the show. Sometimes he'd hand me fifteen bucks and say it was a small crowd, even though I knew we'd had a full house.

"I got sick of that shit and started demanding what I was owed up front. No payment, no music. Simple as that. I still operate that way today."

"At least you solved your problem," said Byrdie.

"Oh, he had other ways of screwing me," said Chuck. "He took writing credit for some of my best songs. When I challenged him, he refused to release the music. Said he'd co-written them with me. The bastard would only promote the songs that he'd given himself publishing rights to."

"Yeah," jumped in Byrdie. "Song writing was where he took advantage of me, too. I aspired to be a songwriter, but didn't know much about the music business. So I got a job as an office assistant for his company, hoping to learn the ropes and maybe even have an inside track.

"Every so often I'd give him one of my original songs to consider. He'd pass on it and tell me to keep working on my craft and that maybe, someday, I'd finally write something worth recording."

"That's pretty standard in the music business," said Sonny. "Songs get passed over all the time. As I'm sure you know from working for him, hundreds of songs are submitted every week and hardly ever do any of them make it onto the air waves."

"That's the problem," said Byrdie. "A couple of my songs, with only a few changes, *did* make it onto the charts. But they were credited to other artists; people and groups I'd never heard of. I didn't get so much as a thank you. The man is a thief!"

"It sounds like I had it pretty good," chimed in Buddy. "I was able to write and record my own songs without his interference. My complaint was the way he treated us when we were on tour. The man refused to spend a cent extra to make our tours comfortable. He'd book us for two shows in the same day, one in the afternoon, another in the evening, in different towns a hundred miles apart, even in the dead of winter. To save money, he'd rent an old school bus to serve as both our transportation and our accommodations. Anything to save a buck. But he always made sure he got his full cut of every performance, whatever the cost to us."

Cher sat quietly listening as the others told of their experiences with Weasel Leech.

"What about you?" Sonny asked his partner. "Did Weasel mess with you?"

"Nobody messes with Cher," she boasted. "He tried, once. Asked me to record a demo track for him as a favor; something that other singers could listen to when deciding what songs to choose. I was just a kid. Much to my surprise, a couple weeks later I heard the song on the radio, just as I recorded it, under another artist's name.

"I stormed over to see him, told him he didn't have the right to do that. That little weasel, and I am not making this up, pulled a gun on me and proclaimed 'I'm Walter Leech, I have the right to do whatever I want!'"

"What'd you do?" asked Chuck.

"I broke out laughing. Told him he wasn't pulling that crap on me and I walked out the door; left the little weasel standing there with his gun in his hand, if ya know what I mean."

"So is that where he got the name Weasel?"

"Absolutely. You mess with Cher, you live to regret it."

Tony couldn't believe what he was hearing. Even though he'd created the characters and scenarios for the dinner guests, he was amazed, and a little bit concerned, how each of them was getting into their character's skin and expanding on what he'd written.

I hope that my whodunit ending still makes sense, he thought. *At the rate these characters are developing, I'm concerned they all might have done it.*

He stepped into the kitchen where Megan was helping Martha prepare the next course.

"I'm glad Weasel isn't actually here," he said. "Any one of these character seems ready to kill him."

Chapter 11

One of the guests, Byrdie, stuck her head in the kitchen, where Tony had joined Megan and Martha. "Just wanted to let you know I'm heading to the little girl's room."

"Okay. It's just down the hall on your right," Tony responded. He knew that he'd specified the rest room as the place for Byrdie to look for a clue, but hadn't expected she'd go there so soon.

"You must have really enjoyed your salad to have eaten it so quickly," Martha commented.

"I'm more of a meat and potatos girl," she responded. "And I don't like mushrooms at all. But I did enjoy the fresh bread and honey."

She headed toward the rest room.

The mystery was taking on a life of its own and Tony would need to keep up with it. He was beginning to worry that the story could get away from him, that he hadn't planted enough clues to match the developing story. When writing the script, he had expected that the guests would try to conceal the clues about their relationships with Weasel. He'd assumed they would want to avoid drawing attention to themselves as being the likely culprit.

He'd assumed wrong.

Instead, their instant dislike for Mr. Leech was so strong that each character seemed hopeful that he or she might be the perpetrator of a crime against him.

Tony turned to Megan.

"When Byrdie gets out of the bathroom, could you steer her back into the dining room?"

His wife nodded, but seemed puzzled by his request.

"Based on what I've been hearing, I need to adjust some of the clues I planted and add a couple more. Could you also try to keep everyone else in the dining room for a few more minutes?"

"I can send her back to the dining room," said Megan. "Any suggestions how I stall the whole group?"

"I don't know. Tell a few murder mystery jokes?"

"Such as... ?"

"How many mystery writers does it take to change a light bulb? Two. One to change the bulb, and the other to give it an unexpected twist at the end."

Megan grimaced. "I'll ask them how they're enjoying their dinner and what they like best about the resort."

"Give me about ten minutes and then you can release them to explore the other rooms."

"I'll do what I can," said Megan.

"While you two are doing that," chimed in Martha, "I'll finish prepping the next course. It'll actually work better if everyone heads out to search for clues at once. Then I can put the food on the table while they're gone and it'll be waiting for them when they return."

The two women watched as Tony stepped across the hall and placed his hand on the door knob to Rudy's private space. He hesitated. A still, small voice inside his conscience told him that he shouldn't be doing this. Subconsciously he hoped the door would be locked.

The knob turned easily.

He quickly stepped inside and closed the door behind him.

A minute ago this had seemed like a good idea. Now, staring at the collection of vintage guitars, he wasn't so sure. If Rudy found out, would he be furious or find it amusing?

Realizing that he had only a few minutes before Megan turned lose the crowd, he quickly assessed the guitars displayed in the corner. He definitely didn't want to mess with the Stratocaster. He selected one that looked the least valuable, picked it up, quickly removed one of the strings and stuck the string in his pocket.

After setting the now five-string guitar back on its stand, he quickly left the room, quietly closing the door behind him.

He hustled up the stairs and down the hall to Guest Room Number Five. On the table next to the bed was a receipt for a peanut butter and banana sandwich.

I gotta love the guy impersonating Elvis, thought Tony. *He jumped right into this stereotype.*

Peeking out from beneath the receipt was a key on an old-school key tag that said Library. He grabbed the key and hurried to the library, which was at the end of the hall, above the dining room.

The door was locked, as expected. Using the key retrieved from Room Five he opened the door and went inside. It was a classic library, with book shelves covering two walls. A large leather chair faced the window. Over the chair's back, Tony could see the top of someone's head.

He hurried around to the front of the chair. Nestled into its luxurious cushions sat a skeleton looking as if he was ready to host an episode of Masterpiece Theater. The skeleton had on a curly black wig, trimmed to just below the top of where his ears should be. A pair of granny glasses rested over the eye holes of his face. He was wearing a black turtleneck under a light blue Nehru jacket with an upturned collar. Around his neck, hanging from a string of love beads, was a multi-colored peace symbol medallion. In his bony hand was a bouquet of fresh foxglove flowers.

Tony quickly wrapped the guitar string around the skeleton's neck, then turned and scanned Rudy's collection of Agatha Christie books. He found what he was looking for—"Murder on the Orient Express"—opened the book and set it on the table beside the skeleton, as if the skeleton had been reading it. Next to the book was an empty mug with a brownish residue in the bottom.

"Thank you for your assistance, Mr. Bones," Tony said to the skeleton.

Mr. Bones was a medical skeleton that Megan and Tony had found the summer before hidden in the spring house behind Blackbird Cabin. Over the years, he had been dressed in various costumes for different occasions. He'd once been Santa Bones; another time he was dressed as the Great Gatsby. Surprisingly, this wasn't the first time he was portraying the victim of a fictitious murder.

Tony quickly left the room, locking the door behind

himself. Then he returned to Room Five, hid the key back under the receipt, and went downstairs.

He could hear some commotion among the guests in the dining room. They seemed to be getting restless.

No time to waste, he thought, hurrying outside and scurrying over to where the cars were parked. He tried to recall which car Janis had arrived in, took his best guess, and began searching the ground around it. He remembered that when she arrived she was smoking a cigarette, but didn't recall seeing her with it on the porch. He searched the ground and, sure enough, found the butt laying not far from the car. He picked it up and carried it to the other side of the lodge, where the foxglove plants were blooming.

Tony had gathered a few of the blooms earlier to place in Mr. Bones' hand and now he went back to the spot where he'd picked them and stripped off a few more leaves so it was obvious that someone had disturbed this spot in the garden. Since Rudy was no longer doing the gardening himself, Tony hoped the old man wouldn't notice. Then he dropped the cigarette butt on the ground next to the disturbed plants.

Got it! he congratulated himself. Then he hurried back into the lodge to monitor how things were progressing.

While he'd been gone, Byrdie had come back from the rest room with a small container in her hand.

"Look what I found," she announced to the whole room. She held up an amber-colored, plastic medicine bottle with a label that read Digitek. "It was in the wastebasket in the bathroom and looks suspicious.

"The date the prescription was filled was only a week

ago," she continued, "but the container is empty. Could be a clue. Does anyone know what Digitek is?"

"Sounds like the name of a computer company," said Sonny. "Maybe it's from one of those new AI pharmacies?"

Cher rolled her eyes, pulled out her phone and quickly corrected him: "It's a medication that treats heart failure and an irregular heartbeat. Also known as digitalis. An overdose can cause death."

"Digitalis?" said Byrdie. "That's the scientific name for foxglove."

Megan noticed Tony appear in the doorway. He gave her a thumbs up.

"This would be a good time for the rest of you to visit your rooms and see what other clues you can find," she announced. "Come back in here in about twenty minutes for your next dinner course. I'll ring the bell again to let you know when it's time to return."

Chapter 12

Rather than follow the instructions to discreetly visit their specified room, as Byrdie had done, the other characters began working together.

"I've got Guest Room Number Three," announced Elvis. "Does anyone else have that room? We could check it out together."

Mama Bass jumped up, waving her note in the air, looking as if her name had just been called to 'come on down' for "Let's Make a Deal."

"I've got Guest Room Number Three!" she shrieked. "What did I win?"

"Let's go find out," said Elvis.

Buddy and Chuck were both assigned to the Library and immediately followed Elvis and Mama up the stairs.

Cher announced that she had the Game Room.

"I'm with you, babe," said Sonny, looking at his paper.

Cher looked right past him and said to Janis, "Want to go check out the Game Room with me?"

Janis looked at the room listed on her paper—Guest Room Number Five—and said, "yup, Game Room it is." She crumpled up her paper and tossed it on the floor. Then she and Cher headed to the room on the opposite side of the Great Hall that housed a ping-pong table, bumper pool table and a vintage bowling machine, as well as shelves filled with puzzles and board games.

Sonny looked out the window at Byrdie, who, having already been to her assigned room, was sitting alone on the porch swing. He bent down and picked up the crumpled paper Janis had tossed on the floor and stuck it in his pocket along with his own room assignment, then went out to join her.

"You did a good job finding that first clue," said Sonny "Okay if I join you out here? We could trade stories about song writing."

"That'd be great," Byrdie responded. "I'd love to get some tips from someone who did it right."

As Byrdie and Sonny talked on the porch, Cher and Janis began searching in the recreation center for anything that might be a clue to what happened to Weasel Leach.

"Since this is a murder mystery dinner," said Cher, "I am going on the assumption that he's dead."

"If he's not dead, he should be," said Janis.

Cher noticed that one of the windows had a broken lock and no screen. On further examination she saw that the screen was laying on the ground outside, among the shrubs surrounding the building.

"This could be how the murderer got in and out," she said.

Janis came over and tried to slide the window up. It opened, but only a few inches. A stop was screwed into the frame limiting how high it could be raised.

"So much for that being the way the murderer got into the lodge," said Cher.

"Maybe the murderer was a really skinny gymnast."

Cher gave her 'that look,' which was usually reserved for Sonny.

"What?" Janis glared back. "Murder mysteries have all kinds of weird suspects."

Cher strutted past the ping-pong table, flicking a ball onto the floor with her finger as she went by, and continued over to the old bowling game that stood in the corner. It was waist high, about ten feet long, with bowling pins hanging down from wires. Instead of bowling balls, the pins were toppled with a heavy chrome puck.

"Have you ever played one of these?" Cher asked.

"Hell yeh. Half the honky tonks we played back in Texas had one. Bar owners liked them cause they didn't take much space and didn't cause as many fights as the pool tables."

Cher picked up the puck.

"It's heavy."

"What'd you expect? You can't bowl with a ping-pong ball."

"And it's kinda gross. I don't think it would slide down the alley very easily."

"Give me that thing."

Janis grabbed the puck from Cher. She looked at it more closely and noticed a reddish-brown substance crusted around the bottom edge of the puck. "Could be dried blood. I think we found our murder weapon!"

Cher took back the puck and looked at it more closely.

"It's rust."

"Blood is high in iron. Iron turns into rust. Weasel Leach was killed in the Game Room with a bowling puck!"

"By who?"

"Who cares as long as he's dead."

Upstairs, Chuck and Buddy were frustrated.

"We can't get into our room," Chuck announced as he and Buddy walked down the hall to Guest Room Number Three to see if Mama and Elvis might have any ideas on how to help them get into the Library.

"How'd you get inside here?" Chuck asked.

"We opened the door," said Mama. "It wasn't locked."

Elvis suggested that they try sliding their hand along the top of the door frame. "That's where they always hide the key in the movies."

Mama and Elvis watched as Buddy and Chuck hurried back to the library door. Buddy reached up and slid his hand along the top of the portal, releasing an avalanche of dust but no key.

"I've got an idea," Elvis called to Chuck and Buddy. He stepped back into Guest Room Number Three and grabbed a gardening magazine that was lying open on the dresser. He took the open magazine down to the library door, dramatically knelt down on one knee like it was his big finish on stage, and slid the magazine most of the way beneath it, directly under the lock.

"What are you doing?" Mama asked.

"In locked door mysteries," Elvis explained, "the door is always locked from the inside with the key still in it. I'll simply push the key out of the keyhole, have it fall onto the magazine, and then I can pull it out and we can unlock the door."

"Good idea," said Buddy.

"Only one problem," said Elvis, studying the old fashioned keyhole. "What do I use to push out the key?"

Buddy took off his glasses and handed them to Elvis.

"Try these."

"You're as bad as my wife," Elvis grumbled. "I can see just fine without glasses."

Buddy took back his glasses, elbowed Elvis out of the way, and poked the end of one of the stems into the old-fashioned keyhole.

Nothing happened. There was no clink of the key hitting the floor.

He pushed it in a little farther.

Nothing.

"Well, it was a good idea," said Buddy, putting his glasses back on, "but I don't think the key is in there."

While this was going on, Tony had been watching from the top of the stairs. Obviously, this was not what was supposed to be happening.

Then he remembered that Janis, who should have gone to Room Five where he'd planted the library key, had inexplicably gone to play games with Cher.

He hurried back down the stairs.

"Sorry to interrupt your game, Janis," he said, "but could I see the note with your room assignment?"

"Sorry. Tossed it. Why?"

"Just wondered if you were in the right room."

Did I not put Guest Room Five in anyone's packet? he wondered. *And why are these two playing ping-pong instead of searching in the room with all of the animal mounts? They're supposed to be discovering the hunting rifle and empty cartridge clues that I placed beneath the big bison and water buffalo heads.*

All of a sudden it dawned on him. *Big. I should have written **Big** Game Room.*

He heard Sonny and Byrdie chatting on the front porch and stepped outside.

"Excuse me for interrupting your conversation," he said, "but I was wondering if I could see the notes you received showing which rooms you should go to."

"I left my note on the table," said Byrdie, "but I had the Rest Room. That's where I found the pill bottle."

Sonny pulled two notes out of his pocket, one smooth, one crumpled.

Tony looked confused.

"This one was mine," Sonny said, showing him the pristine note that said Game Room.

"And the other one?"

"I picked it up off the floor," he said, "where Janis tossed it."

He handed the note to Tony, who uncrumpled it and read aloud: "Guest Room Number Five."

"How about you think of this note as your own," said Tony, "and check out Room Number Five? They could really use your help upstairs."

"Okay," said Sonny, getting up from the old metal chair. "I've been feeling kind of useless, anyway. Byrdie, want to join me?"

As the two headed up the wooden staircase, Tony made a quick stop in the kitchen to see how things were going with Megan and Martha.

"Everything going okay in here?"

"Yup. Right on schedule. We should be ready to put the food out in about fifteen minutes. How are things going with the suspects? You look frustrated."

"I thought writing the story would be the hardest part of this event. Nope. The hardest part is watching 'my' characters go off script. Seriously, I have no idea where this is going."

"Isn't improvisation supposed to be half the fun of a mystery dinner?" asked Martha.

"Maybe for the guests."

"It'll be fine," said Megan, giving him a quick kiss. "One more course to go and then it'll be time for the big reveal in the Great Hall. An hour from now we'll all be packing up to head home."

"I'd better go upstairs to see if they've figured out how to get into the Library."

Sonny and Byrdie were inside Room Number Five when Tony stepped into the hall.

Down the hall, Buddy had just pulled the magazine out from under the library door and noticed it was book marked open to an article about growing foxglove. The bookmark was an empty Swiss Miss packet.

"Do you think this might be important?" he asked.

Before anyone could answer, they heard Sonny's voice.

"Hey, Elvis," he called from inside Room Number Five. "I think this must be your room. There's a receipt in here for a peanut butter and banana sandwich."

Byrdie noticed the key under the receipt, grabbed it and hurried out the door. "I think this might be what you need to get into the Library," she called. "Catch."

Chapter 13

"Welcome back for your third course," said Megan as the guests returned to their seats in the Dining Room. "I trust that everyone is having fun searching for clues and trying to deduce who killed Weasel Leach.

"This course is potluck style with a Northwoods flair. On the buffet table you will find two different kinds of lasagna—venison and vegetarian; a delicious green bean casserole, made with fresh-picked green beans; buttered beets; two kinds of potato salad—Grama's and German; and Sheboygan-style hard rolls.

"Feel free to discuss the mystery while you dine. When you've finished eating, you're invited to wander the grounds and relax. I'll ring the bell when it's time to gather in the Great Hall, where you'll find cookies and lemonade."

Tony added: "One more thing. In the small envelope that you received earlier, you'll find a form that you can use to accuse the person you believe killed Mr. Leach and reveal how and why it was done. Fill this out individually, put it back in the envelope, and be sure to bring it with you when we gather in the Great Hall. There should be a pencil in your envelope. Enjoy your meal. See you in the Great Hall in about half an hour."

Tony and Megan stepped into the hallway.

"Are you feeling any less stressed?" she asked. "Everyone seems to be enjoying themselves."

"Let's just say, I'm looking forward to this event being over."

"All for a good cause, right?"

"Right," said Tony taking a deep breath. "I need to remember that our goal is to support the library; a place where a person can enjoy a great mystery by a competent writer instead of fretting over a mystery that seems as if it's being written spontaneously by a committee."

"Not just any committee," Megan grinned. "A committee of characters that you created."

"They're not exactly how I imagined them."

"All the better. The best part of a mystery is the surprise ending, right? Which means, the best is yet to come ... even for you! Maybe this is your payback for refusing to tell me who did it."

"Which, I'm realizing was a good idea. No matter who it turns out to be, I won't have to admit if I got it wrong. I do have to admit, though, that I am extremely curious to see how they decide who dunnit. The participants didn't even find all of the clues I planted, but they did find a few I didn't leave."

"What clues did they miss?"

Tony told her about the rifle and casings in the Big Game Room and the cigarette butt on the ground where the foxglove flowers had been picked.

"I'm hoping they'll still find that one when they're strolling the grounds after they eat."

"I'll see if I can help steer them toward it."

"Thanks."

"Do you want to grab a little something to tide you over while the others are eating? We've got plenty of food."

"No, but thank you. It'll be more relaxing to pick up a pizza on the way home and leisurely enjoy it with a bottle of ice-cold Spotted Cow, at our very own murder mystery cabin."

The dinner conversation was lively and everyone seemed to be enjoying themselves. Rather than eyeing each other suspiciously, the guests appeared unified in their dislike for Weasel Leach. The characters made up increasingly horrific stories about the way he treated them, well beyond the info provided by Tony in their character bios.

While the guests were eating, Tony went upstairs to make sure everything was in order. He figured since no one needed to go up there again, he might as well remove the props and straighten the rooms.

He began in Guest Room Number Three. He picked up the gardening magazine, then dropped it and the empty Swiss Miss packet into his satchel. He quickly scanned the room for anything else that didn't belong there and left, closing the door behind him.

Next he visited Guest Room Number Five. He put the sandwich receipt in his satchel. Then he removed the Library key from the fob, dropped the fob in with the receipt and, after a quick glance around the room, closed the door. He took the key down the hall and after opening the Library door, placed it back where he'd first found it, above the dusty door frame, right where Elvis had pre-dicted it would be.

The Library, which was the scene of the crime, took the most work to straighten up. First he returned "Mur-der On The Orient Express" to the book shelf where it belonged.

This is my fail safe clue, he thought, glad that he decid-ed to add it at the last minute. *If the mystery ends up the way it appears to be heading, I can point to this clue and make it appear as if that's what I had intended all along; that everyone was involved in the murder. No one needs to know that I planted this halfway through to cover my butt.*

He placed the empty hot chocolate mug in his satchel, along with the bouquet of foxglove flowers.

He decided that it would be easiest to leave Mr. Bones dressed for the ride home, but as soon as he tried to pick him up the guitar string sprung off his neck and flew onto the floor.

Glad that didn't happen when people were in here. It could have poked out someone's eye.

He rolled up the string, twisted it together so it wouldn't pop apart again, and put it in his pocket.

After slinging the satchel over his shoulder, he carried Mr. Bones down the hall to the back stairway and out to his car. On the drive to the lodge, the skeleton had ridden in the passenger seat, which had caused a few puzzled looks from nearby vehicles. This time, he'd need to be in the back, since Megan would be riding home with him.

While Tony was cleaning out the upstairs rooms, Me-gan helped Martha pack up the things from the meal.

Martha had agreed to take all of the dishes home with her to sort out and wash, since they didn't want to mess up Rudy's kitchen.

"How about I package up some of the extra food and leave it in the fridge for Rudy?" Martha suggested. "We're going to have enough leftovers."

"Sounds like a good idea. He'll probably appreciate it."

Megan noticed that the conversation in the Dining Room was thinning out and the guests were beginning to go outside.

"I think I should go wander around in the yard and see if I can steer someone to one of the clues that hasn't yet been found."

"Okay. I can start cleaning things up in the Dining Room as soon as everyone's out of there. The cookies and lemonade will take only a minute to set up in the Great Hall."

Tony had just finished getting Mr. Bones situated in the back seat when he noticed the guests starting to wander around the yard. He quickly tossed a blanket over the 'murder victim' so no one would notice him if they wandered near the car.

Megan strolled around the grounds, looking for the cigarette butt. She scanned the flowers and easily discovered the spot where the foxglove flowers had been picked, but she didn't see any butts lying on the ground nearby. She noticed Tony by the car and joined him.

"Was there more than one place where you picked the flowers?" she asked him. "I didn't see any cigarette butt where I was looking."

"No, just one spot, pretty close to the lake."

"That's where I looked, but I couldn't find anything. I don't want to steer someone to the spot if the clue isn't there."

"Maybe someone already picked it up?"

"I haven't seen anyone in that part of the yard. I came out here as soon as the guests started leaving the Dining Room."

"Odd. Maybe a Blue Jay or chipmunk dragged it away."

"If that's the case, you'll have to add a bird and a rodent to your list of suspects," she teased.

Tony just shook his head. "Thanks for trying. I don't think that another missed clue will make much of a difference, anyway, based on how things are going."

A few minutes later, Megan rang the bell. It was time for the suspects to gather in the Great Hall for the big reveal.

Chapter 14

"Welcome back," said Megan. "Grab a cookie and a glass of lemonade before you sit down. You might want to shift the chairs around so we're in more of a circle."

Once everyone was settled, she continued.

"Did everyone bring their completed accusation sheets?"

A few held them up, others simply nodded. For the first time all evening, no one said a word.

The portrait of Weasel Leach was now sitting on the fireplace mantel. He peered down menacingly at the suspects, almost daring them to say aloud what they'd done to him.

"Weasel, Weasel, Weasel," Megan began, looking up at his picture. "We know what you've been up to, you naughty boy. You've really ticked off the folks in this room with your shenanigans. So much so, that someone decided to do... you... in.

"But who? Who would want to knock off a sweet guy like you?"

She slowly scanned the faces of the suspects, from one to another, then said almost as an aside: "Like I said before, you all look pretty guilty."

A few folks chuckled.

"We're about to find out who killed Weasel Leach and how it was done. We're counting on you, each one of you, to tell us who you believe the killer was and how. To get started, please have your accusation sheet handy."

"What's our prize if we get it right?" asked Janis.

"Your prize, Dearie" said Cher, "was getting to spend more time with me. What else could you want?"

Sonny had a hard time to keep from laughing.

"Your prize for getting it right," Megan said, "is the satisfaction of knowing that you are an ace detective."

"How about cookies and a juice box for everyone?" suggested Elvis. "That way we will all feel like winners."

"Duh," said Buddy. "Look what's on the table. Cookies and lemonade. All you're missing is the box."

"That brings up a *real* mystery," interjected Mama. "What's the secret to getting that stupid straw into the juice box without squirting it all over yourself? And why is the straw so short?"

"Would anyone like to begin reading their accusation?" Megan asked, trying to regain control. "Chuck, how about you? Who do you think killed Weasel Leach?"

Chuck opened his form and read: "I am accusing Mama Bass. She poisoned Weasel with something in his hot chocolate. The empty mug was found next to his chair and the empty Swiss Miss packet was found in her room."

Then he added spontaneously: "But I think Mama was probably too high to pull it off herself, so I think that she had help from Byrdie, who we all saw holding the empty pill bottle."

"I'm the one who *found* the pill bottle," said Byrdie defensively. "If I'd have poisoned him I certainly wouldn't have shown the bottle to everyone."

"Very clever way to deflect attention," said Chuck. "But I still think you had a hand in it."

"I'm with you, Chuck," said Cher. "Byrdie was Mama's accomplice."

She pointed out that Byrdie was the one who not only found the pill container, but knew that foxglove was the same poison as the digitalis in the prescription.

"Next," said Megan, "let's hear friom Elvis. Who do you accuse?"

"I think that Weasel Leach was nuthin' but a hound dog, and I'd liked to have killed him myself. Is that an acceptable answer?"

Megan looked to Tony, who was standing in the doorway.

"Well," Tony said, scratching his head, "I guess there's nothing in the rules that says you can't accuse yourself."

"If he confesses, does that mean the mystery is solved, game over?" asked Buddy.

"Don't worry," said Tony. "We'll let the rest of you weigh in. Maybe he's incriminating himself in order to protect another person."

"Elvis," Megan continued, "how did you kill Mr. Leach?"

He glanced at Buddy, then said: "I strangled him with a guitar string, Ma'am. Twisted it right around his weasely little neck, yes, that's what I did. With a guitar string."

"Buddy," Megan said, "would you like to tell us who you believe killed Weasel?"

Buddy looked at Elvis, but didn't say a word.

Megan tried again: "Just read to us what you've written on your paper."

Buddy opened the page and read: "'The murderer was Elvis, who did it with a guitar string.' But I want to change my vote," he stammered. "I can't let Elvis take the rap for Weasel's murder. I did it. It was all my idea. I killed him with the guitar string."

"Interesting," said Cher. "I've seen this tactic in the movies. Two people both confess to the same crime, the jury gets confused and they both go free. Well played boys, well played."

"Who do you think did it, Cher?" Megan asked.

"That's easy," she said, looking at her accusation sheet. "The murder was committed by Sonny. He bored Weasel to death by reading to him from that Agatha Christie book found next to the body. Seriously, that story goes on and on and on and in the end it turns out that they all did it. Poor Agatha obviously ran out of ideas and just threw in the towel."

"I'm with Cher," jumped in Janis, "Sonny's the one who knew where the key was for the Library. He's the only one who could have gotten in to kill him."

"That's only 'cause Janis cheated," Sonny said, defending himself. "I'll bet she's the murderer! She improperly went to the Game Room with Cher instead of to Room Five, like she was supposed to."

"Room Five was where Elvis was staying," said Byrdie. "We found the receipt for his sandwich in that room."

"Or so you say," said Janis, pointing a finger at Sonny. "For some nefarious reason he decided to go to Room

Five even though his instructions clearly said that he was to go to the Game Room."

"That's cause you jumped in and went to..." mumbled Sonny.

"Time to come clean, Sonny?" Cher said. "Tell everyone how you lied about your assigned room rather than having to spend time with me in the Game Room!"

"I, I..."

Megan interrupted. "Janis, does that mean that you wrote down that Sonny was the murderer?"

"Absolutely," she said, crumpling her accusation form and sticking it in her pocket. "He hated Weasel. While the rest of us were searching for clues in our assigned rooms, he snuck outside, gathered some poisonous foxglove and snuck it into Weasel's drink. The rest of us were so busy searching for clues in the rooms that we were assigned, no one noticed what he was up to."

Birdie raised her hand.

Megan nodded to her.

"I was with Sonny the whole time. I can vouch for him. We didn't leave the porch and he certainly didn't go into the flower bed to pick a poisonous plant."

Cher jumped back into the fray: "Obviously, Byrdie was Sonny's accomplice and is trying to protect him. Together they poisoned him with a mixture of foxglove leaves and Digitek tablets."

"I thought you said Byrdie was *my* accomplice," said Mama. "Byrdie, were you cheating on me with Sonny?"

Megan tried to regain control: "Birdie, we haven't heard your accusation yet. Who do you think killed Weasel Leach?"

"Sorry," she said, looking directly at Cher, "but I think you murdered him. You and Chuck and Buddy have all tried to shift blame away from yourselves by accusing me."

"And just how did *I* murder him?" asked Cher.

"You strangled him."

"Buddy and Chuck have already confessed to strangling him with the guitar string. That lane's been taken."

"You didn't strangle him with the guitar string," explained Byrdie. "You strangled him with the chain on his peace and love medallion. A medallion that you gave him years ago. A medallion that he was wearing tonight to spite you. Deep down, you loved the man; loved him enough to give him a nickname. But he wouldn't return your love, he was only in it for the money."

Cher just rolled her eyes.

"It was a crime of passion!" Byrdie continued. "You hadn't seen him for years, but when you saw him wearing the medallion, the old spark burst into flame. You looked into his eyes, put your hands around his neck and leaned in to give him a kiss. But he pulled away. You felt the silver chain of his medallion sliding through your fingers. You'd given him that medallion as a symbol of your love, but now he wore it to mock you.

"You clutched the chain and pulled it tighter and tighter and tighter until he collapsed into his chair."

Byrdie scanned the faces of the others in the room.

"If you look closely at the bruises on Weasel's neck, you'll see that the marks were made from the links of the chain, not the thin line that a guitar string would have caused. Weasel Leach was already dead by the time Chuck and Buddy arrived on the scene. They had planned to murder him themselves, so for good measure they wrapped the string around his neck anyway.

"Ladies and gentlemen of the jury, the murderer was Cher! I rest my case."

The rest of the room, including Cher, burst into spontaneous applause.

Byrdie stepped back and took a bow.

Megan looked to her husband for a clue on what to do next. He was the only one who knew the solution he'd written into the script.

"I think we have a winner!" Tony announced quickly, stepping into the circle. He looked relieved. "How about another round of applause for Byrdie Finch! And a big thanks to all of you. We couldn't have done it without you. Cookies and juice for all!"

"Thank you everyone for participating in this event," Megan said when the applause died down. "Have a safe drive home."

Chapter 15

"We survived!" said Tony, high-fiving Megan and Martha. "Good job."

While the murderer was being unmasked in the Great Hall, Martha had been busy clearing away the rest of the dishes and packing things up to take home.

"Do you want the left-over cookies," she asked, "or should we leave them for Rudy? I think he'll probably enjoy them."

"Sure, leave them for him," said Megan.

"We ended up with a lot more salad greens than I expected, too," Martha said. "I bagged them up and put them in the refrigerator. I believe you mentioned that Rudy likes to use them for smoothies."

"They came from his garden," said Megan, "so I guess they're technically his."

"I also left him the last piece of lasagna."

"Could you return the baking dishes to the others?" Megan asked.

"Sure thing. I'll see them next weekend at the Courthouse Square Arts Festival. We'll have a Friends table there to pass out info about the library's building project. Tony, do you think you'll have the brochures ready for us to distribute?"

Tony grimaced: "I was hoping to have them completed by now, but seems like I kinda got drafted into writing a murder mystery script. I still need to show the pictures to Rudy, so he can decide which ones we should use. I'll see if I can get the brochure done this week. I'll be at the festival, too, selling my 'Secret of Blackbird Cabin' book. If I have the brochures done, I'll bring them along."

"Thanks for all the work you two have put into the dinner," Martha said as she headed for her car. "As you told the dinner guests, we couldn't have done it without you."

"Well," said Megan when she and Tony were ready to head out to their car, "this has been fun."

Tony did a quick check around the lodge to make sure all of the lights were turned off, then he locked the front door and hid the key under the stone frog, as Rudy had requested.

"I ordered the pizza," Megan said when Tony got in the car. "It should be ready for us to pick up by the time we get there."

"Fantastic," said Tony. "I'm ready to relax, just the two of us, in our quiet little cabin. You did a great job as host, by the way. Nice bit of drama there at the end."

"Why thank you," she smiled, reaching over and touching his hand. "And you did a very nice job with the script. One question: Is that the solution to the murder that you had expected?"

"I'll never tell."

Fifteen minutes later they pulled into Pizza Hideaway.

Tony jumped out and went inside to pick up the pizza. They were just taking it out of the oven.

"Great service," he said as they slid it into a large, flat, paper bag. He reached into his pocket for his wallet only to be poked by something sharp.

The guitar string.

"Megan," he said as he handed her the pizza. "We need to go back to the lodge. I forgot to put the string back on Rudy's guitar."

"Can't it wait until tomorrow? The pizza will get cold."

"Sorry. I don't want him to find out that I removed it. It won't take me long to put it back on. Then I can relax and enjoy the rest of the evening."

The lodge was still dark when they pulled up. *Good,* thought Tony, *he hasn't come back yet.*

Tony hurried out of the car, retrieved the key from under the stone frog and went inside.

He made his way through the dark Great Hall, flipped on the light in the hallway and opened the door leading to Rudy's private residence. Illuminated only by the light from the hallway, he picked up the guitar and quickly replaced the missing string.

When he was ready to set it back down, he noticed that there were two empty guitar stands. The stand closest to him was for the guitar that he held in his hand.

The other empty stand was for Rudy's irreplaceable, love-of-his-life, vintage Stratocaster.

I am so screwed.

A few minutes later, Megan heard a tap on her car window. It was a very upset looking Tony.

"Megan, you need to come in the lodge and help me search for Rudy's guitar."

"What? The guitar you took the string from?"

"No. His prized Stratocaster. It's not on the stand in his room."

"Maybe he packed it away before we all got here, or took it with him."

"No, I'm sure it was there when I took the string off the other guitar. Someone must have taken it during the dinner."

Megan got out of the car and hurried into the lodge with her husband.

"I'll look upstairs," he said. "You check down here. I already searched his room, but another set of eyes in there wouldn't hurt. The case is still in the closet, so the guitar was probably grabbed quickly."

They opened every closet door, looked behind every couch and peered beneath every bed. No luck.

"Now what?" Megan asked when they finished their search. "Do we call the police?"

Tony thought a moment, then replied, "I think we need to tell Rudy, first. We'll let him decide."

"Maybe he came back while we were getting the pizza and then took it with him."

"We can hope."

"Did he say when he'd be back?"

"No, he didn't even say where he was going."

Tony took a small notebook and pen out of the glove box and wrote Rudy a note, explaining what happened and asking that he get in contact with them as soon as he got back. He stuck it on the door to Tony's room, where he'd find it before he went inside.

"Let's wait here for awhile," suggested Megan. "Hopefully he'll be back soon and we can tell him what happened in person."

They watched the moon's reflection move across the lake as they sat silently on the porch eating their pizza. It wasn't quite the relaxing meal they'd been looking forward to.

"I don't think he's coming back tonight," Tony finally said, breaking the silence. "We might as well go back to the cabin and get some sleep. Hopefully he'll call us in the morning."

Chapter 16

By ten the next morning, they hadn't heard from Rudy.

"Do you suppose he went away for the weekend?" Megan wondered.

"Could be. Since he didn't return last night, that would make sense."

"How about we get a few things done around here this morning, then drive over to the lodge and see if he's come home?"

"Sounds like a plan. I'd like to get the yard mowed before it gets too hot. I've been putting it off while working on the murder mystery. Now that that's done, life can get back to normal."

"On the way over to the lodge," Megan said, "let's stop at the nursery to see if they have some of those foxglove plants that Rudy suggested. It'd be great to finally have some flowers that don't get eaten by the deer."

Tony was amazed at how much the mowed area around the cabin—it didn't quite qualify for being called a lawn—had grown up in the past two weeks. When they bought the cabin, the cleared area was nearly grown over with tall grass, small balsam trees and maple saplings. He'd expanded the area to restore more of the meadow that was originally in front of the cabin. He was pleasantly surprised at the number of wildflowers that had come back.

When mowing—he'd recently gone all out and purchased a brand-new, bright-yellow riding mower—he carefully avoided the areas in bloom, leaving islands of daisies, orange hawkweed and milkweed.

The new mower made his task much easier and a lot more fun. He was planning to expand and widen the trail around the lake this summer, as well. The narrow path along the shore made for a pleasant little stroll, but it was still a bit on the rugged side. Megan wasn't a fan of clambering over the occasional downed tree or being brushed against by the overreaching branches in the narrower sections. His plan was to get the trail wide enough and level enough so that he could use the mower to keep it clear. Other folks in the area drove their ATVs through the woods. Tony had his Cub Cadet.

They got to Foxglove Lodge about two o'clock. They still hadn't heard from Rudy and no one answered when they knocked on the door.

"Do you think we should go in?" asked Tony.

"Why?"

"I'd like to see if the note is still on his door."

Megan shrugged her shoulders.

Tony tipped up the side of the stone frog to get to the key. It wasn't there.

"That's odd," he said. "I'm sure I put it back. You saw me, right?"

"I saw you put it back the first time, but when you went

back in to replace the guitar string, I stayed in the car. Check again."

Tony lifted the frog again, this time completely off the ground. Still no key. He began searching around the area. He even lifted up a few decorative rocks surrounding the statue in case he'd mistaken one of them for the stone frog in the dark. Still no key.

"That's very weird," he said under his breath. He peered into the Great Hall through the window. Everything looked the same as he remembered it from the night before.

"Any suggestions?" he called to his wife, who had wandered over to look at the foxglove plants so she'd know what to buy at the nursery.

"I guess we'll just have to wait for his call. We might as well go."

On Sunday evening Tony's phone rang. It was Rudy. He'd just returned home and found the note on his door. He had gone up to Bayfield for the weekend to see a performance by a group of old musicians, a couple of which he knew.

Tony quickly told him about the missing guitar. Not surprisingly, Rudy had already noticed that it was missing. Tony could tell by the tone of Rudy's voice, that he was upset.

"I feel just awful about this," said Tony, "and I'd really like to help you figure out what happened to it. Would it be okay if I come by first thing in the morning?"

Tony pulled up to Foxglove Lodge bright and early the

next morning. Megan had said he should at least give Rudy time to eat his breakfast before he arrived, but Tony didn't want to waste any time helping the old man get his guitar back. He had a couple of ideas where to look for it, but he didn't want to proceed without Tony's approval.

Rudy was sitting on the porch when Tony pulled up.

"So, how did your murder mystery dinner go?" Rudy called with a bit of a chuckle. "Any surprises?"

"During or after the dinner?"

"Both. Start with the dinner. Then we can talk about the guitar."

Tony gave him a brief overview of the event. He was going to omit the part about taking the string off Rudy's other guitar, but realized that without that detail it wouldn't make any sense why Tony had gone into Rudy's private space and discovered the guitar was missing.

"I feel really, really bad about this," Tony said. "It was so generous of you to allow us the use of your lodge to hold the event. I never should have gone into your room. This wouldn't have happened if I hadn't decided to borrow one of your guitar strings."

"You don't know that. If you hadn't come back to replace the string, you wouldn't even have known the guitar went missing. It wouldn't have been discovered until I returned last night. This way, we can narrow down the time it was taken to just a couple of hours, instead of a couple of days."

"But I never shoulda..."

"Did you unlock the door to my room?"

"No, it wasn't locked."

"So, you're telling me," he said loudy, striking his cane

on the porch floor for emphasis, "that some doofus allowed a whole group of strangers to come into his house, wander around from room to room, unsupervised, and didn't even have the common sense to lock the door to the one room that contained his most valuable items?"

"That's not exactly how I'd have put it."

"Let's just leave it at that and figure out how to move on," Rudy said calmly. "Oh, one other thing. The guitar wasn't the only thing taken. My toothbrush is missing. You must have had one hell of a weird party."

"A question," Tony asked cautiously. "Was the guitar insured?"

"It was. About a dozen years ago I had the frets dressed and the electronics given a complete cleaning at Doug's Guitar Shop in La Crosse."

"I know that shop," said Tony. "Been there several times. Doug's got one of the best private collections of vintage electric guitars anywhere. Some amazing instruments, especially in his private collection. All you have to do to see his collection is ask."

"He's also one of the top appraisers of electric guitars in the country. I had him appraise mine so I'd have a value for insuring it."

"I almost hate to ask, but what's it valued at?"

"To me, it's invaluable. But for a collector of vintage instruments, Doug appraised it, in its original case, at $50,000. Probably worth more today."

"So someone knew what they were taking."

"Maybe, maybe not. They left the case in the closet. Which is a good thing, since that's where I'd stored my valuable papers, including the appraisal."

"Maybe, then," said Tony optimistically, "the thief doesn't know what it's worth and will try to sell it on online or pawn it. How about we check out the music store and a couple of pawn shops to alert them to watch for it. Have you had breakfast?"

"I was about to pick some raspberries and make a smoothie with them and the greens that I found in the fridge. I could make one for you, too."

"How about I buy you breakfast at Pappy's Cafe? It's just across from the pawn shop. Megan says they've got the best omelettes in town. I owe you."

"I guess the smoothie can wait. One request. While we're out, could we stop at Dollar Tree? Seems that I need a new toothbrush."

"How did your visit with Rudy go?" Megan asked when Tony returned to the cabin. "Is he pretty upset?"

"Not as much as I expected. He obviously wasn't happy, but the man has a really positive outlook on life. I hope that when I'm his age, I'll be as pleasant."

"No need to wait until then," she joked.

Tony explained how they'd gone to the music store and pawn shops in town to ask them to keep an eye out for the purloined Stratocaster.

"I took him out for a late breakfast at Pappy's when we were done," he said.

"You should have come back and taken me along. You know I like Pappy's and I'd like to get to know Rudy a little better. Martha made several comments about how he seems like such a nice guy."

"I thought about calling you, but Blackbird Cabin

wasn't exactly on the way."

"Good point."

"Here's an alternative," Tony suggested. "I'd like to go to the pawn shops and music stores outside of town to talk with them, too. Even though Rudy isn't blaming me for the guitar being stolen, I do feel a certain responsibility to help him get it back. Want to make a day of it? You and I? We could grab a sub and enjoy it in one of the parks."

"That sounds like fun, as long as we include a few thrift and antique stores, too. Let's plan on that for tomorrow."

The couple spent the rest of the day working in their yard and woods. Megan figured out where to plant her new foxglove plants and discovered how hard it is to dig through sod and roots to create a new bed.

Tony continued his work on widening the trail around the lake. The nice part about such a project was that he could easily see what he'd accomplished. Considering that just a year ago there was only a deer trail around the lake, he was pleased with how far along his trail system was coming. *Next thing you know,* he thought, *I'll be adding spurs and will need to put up some "You Are Here" directional signs.* But that would be for another day. Most likely, for another summer.

Chapter 17

Two days later, Tony and Megan stopped at the library. Megan had a couple of books she needed to return and Tony wanted to run the draft of the charitable gifts brochure past the library director for final approval. The print shop would need it by the end of the day if there was any chance of having it ready to pass out on Saturday at the art fair.

The director thought it looked great. The only thing Tony still needed to do was get Rudy's approval for the pictures he'd chosen. After the fiasco with the guitar, he really hoped that the old rocker was still agreeable to be featured.

As they were about to leave, the librarian at the circulation desk motioned them over.

"I heard you say you were going over to Rudy's. He usually stops by every Tuesday morning to pick up the books he's put on hold, but yesterday he didn't show up. Could you remind him that he's got several books on the shelf that'll be sent back if not picked up soon?"

"Sure, we could do that," said Tony.

"We could take them over to him," offered Megan.

The librarian thought for a moment.

"We're not in the habit of letting someone else take out a patron's books. Privacy is really important."

"We kinda owe him a favor," Megan said. "I'm sure he'll appreciate the gesture. Especially since it's probably because of the library's mystery dinner that he forgot to come by and pick them up."

"Well," said the librarian, considering their offer, "since I know both of you, I guess I can make an exception."

The librarian collected three books from the hold shelf and brought them to the front desk.

As the librarian checked out the books to Rudy, he said: "Sometimes I think he puts titles on hold just so he has a reason to stop by every week to pick them up. He never uses the self-checkout, always brings them to the desk. We've gotten to be friends. Tell him I missed seeing him yesterday."

He handed the books to Megan, who glanced at the titles.

"Looks like he's a fan of cozy murder mysteries," she said.

"That he is. He's always asking for recommendations by new authors. I recommended your Blackbird Cabin book to him," he said to Tony.

"Thank you," said Tony, flattered. "I hope he enjoyed it."

"I'm sure he did. And thank you for delivering these to him. I know he'll appreciate it."

"Happy to help," Megan replied. "Like I said, we owe him a favor after he let us host the mystery dinner at his lodge. You might have heard what happened with his guitar."

"Yes," said the librarian. "My friend from the music store said you'd asked him to be on the lookout for it. We all feel really bad about that."

As they drove to Foxglove Lodge, Megan said: "Martha was asking quite a few questions about Rudy the other night and I realized that I know very little about the man. I was surprised that she didn't know more about him, since she's the one who suggested we ask to use his lodge for the dinner. What do you know about the mystery man?"

"Only what he's told me. I know he was a rock star in the early sixties, then switched careers and made his money in medical technology."

"How about family? Does he have any kids?"

"None that he mentioned. He was widowed about twenty years ago. Ten years after that he had a heart attack and was told he needed to take it easy. That's when he decided to buy the resort."

"So much for taking it easy. It's a lot of work just keeping up our little cabin."

"He's got some fond memories of Foxglove Lodge from when he was young; playing here with his band, falling in love, writing a song about the girl of his dreams. You know, the usual reasons folks retire to their cabin on the lake."

"So, when are you going to write a love song about the girl of your dreams?"

Tony just smiled.

As they passed the golf course and meandered down the long drive to the resort, Megan commented: "Seems like Rudy'd be awfully lonely out here. I wouldn't want to live in Blackbird Cabin if I didn't have you to enjoy it with me. I can see why he appreciates the personal contact he gets at the library."

"The only people he seems to have regular contact with out here are a young couple staying in that cottage," Tony said, pointing to a small lakeside cabin that could barely be seen through the trees. "He mentioned that they stop in every couple of days to say 'hi' and make sure that he's doing okay."

"It's nice that he has someone nearby that he can depend on."

"They tend his yard and gardens in exchange for living in the cabin. Seems like a pretty good deal for both of them."

"It'd be fun to get to know Rudy better. Maybe we can hang around for a while after we give him his books and you show him the pictures. I'd love to hear some stories about his days in Rudy and the Rockets."

Tony knocked on the screen door's wooden frame. The inside door was open.

"Hello, Rudy?" he called when there was no response to his knocking. "Anybody here?"

Still no response.

"At least we know he's home," Megan said. "He wouldn't have gone away without locking the door, especially after having his guitar ripped off."

"He's probably out in the yard somewhere. It's too nice of a day to be cooped up indoors. How about we take a stroll along the lake and see if we can find him?"

"Sounds like a good idea. You can show me the rest of the resort."

They set the books and pictures on the porch railing and headed toward the lake.

"This is gorgeous out here," Megan said as they strolled hand in hand along the foxglove-covered shoreline. "I didn't get much of a chance to enjoy it when we were here for the dinner. It's so much more tranquil today than it was then."

"No kidding. That was one of the least relaxing evenings I've spent. If you ever volunteer me to write another murder mystery script, remind me to say 'no.'"

"But think how easy it would be the next time, now that you've got one under your belt. You know what they say, 'the second time's the charm.'"

"I think it's the third time. Anyway, I have no plans to get past number one."

They passed by the row of old cabins that Tony had pointed out on the way in, but didn't see anyone around the cottage occupied by the young couple. The other two buildings had obviously sat empty for many years.

When they reached the bend in the path, Tony said: "Now you're in for a surprise."

"Wow," she said as the two-story boat house appeared through the trees, stretching out over the lake. "Does someone live in there?"

"You'll see."

The door was locked. Tony remembered where the key was hidden, but decided against unlocking it.

He tried to peer inside through the glass in the door, but couldn't see much beyond the back of the stage.

"Actually, I guess you won't see. Sorry. There's a really cool dance hall in there. Stars on the ceiling, little tables along the windows, the whole nine yards. This is where Rudy's band played. We'll have to come back another time when he can give you his guided tour. I'm surprised we haven't run into him, yet."

Megan noticed a stairway along the side of the building leading down toward the lake.

"Let's go down there."

Before he could respond she was halfway to the bottom. A door at the bottom of the stairs led into the lower level of the boathouse. It wasn't locked.

Megan opened it and peered into a large, garage-like room over the water. It took a minute to adjust her eyes to the unusual light. The boat house was open on the lake side and the sunlight reflecting off the slow, rhythmic waves had a slightly disorienting, yet weirdly calming effect. Three docks jutted out from a long, wooden walkway that ran along the back wall.

"This must have been quite a resort in its day," Megan said, standing with her hands against the back wall. Another door at the far end of the walkway was cracked open.

"Where's that go?"

"It goes up to the dance hall."

"Good," she said, walking to the door."Then we can get in from down here." She grabbed the handle and pulled it all the way open. Just inside the door, on the left, was a stairway leading up.

"That would go to the ballroom," said Tony. "Rudy showed me where it comes out behind the curtain at the back of the stage."

"What about that door?" she said, noting the portal straight ahead of her.

The door was open a crack, unlike when Rudy showed the boat house to Tony. Megan pulled it open all the way. The web-covered, bare light bulbs inside the tunnel were lit. They were so dirty that the light they produced looked like something created for a haunted house.

"That would be the tunnel that inspired Rudy's song 'Tunnel of Love.'"

"Looks more like something that would have inspired Michael Jackson's 'Thriller.'"

"It's actually not as bad as I imagined" Tony said, peering into the space. "Rudy told me it was so filled up with spider webs that you couldn't pass through without getting covered with them. It's disgusting, but I don't see any webs actually blocking the tunnel."

"It looks like someone's gone through here recently and brushed them aside," Megan observed, noting the strands of broken web hanging from the walls onto the tunnel floor.

"In that case, should we go through the tunnel and see where it comes out?"

"No," she responded quickly, giving him a look that said *why would you even imagine I'd want to do that?* "But I would like to see what's upstairs."

"Since we've come this far, we might as well."

Tony led the way to the top of the stairs and stopped in the small space behind the curtain at the back of the stage.

When Megan was beside him, he grabbed the edge of

the curtain and proclaimed in his best announcer voice: "Ladies and gentlemen, welcome to the Starlight Ballroom!"

He pulled aside the curtain and Megan let out a scream.

Crumpled over the edge of the stage was Rudy, his head and right arm hanging down onto the dance floor, his cane on the stage behind him, just beyond his reach. They quickly rushed to his side. A pool of blood surrounded his head like a macabre halo.

He wasn't moving.

Megan's experience working in a hospital years ago clicked in and she quickly checked for a pulse. It was weak. He was alive but unresponsive.

"Should we turn him over?" Tony asked.

Megan shook her head.

Tony immediately dialed 911.

It appeared that the old man had tripped and landed face first against the edge of the stage. The blood surrounding his head seemed to have come from his mouth and nose. It was already dried. He'd obviously been here for some time.

Tony handed the phone to Megan, then hurried down the stairs, through the boat house, up the outer staircase and out to the driveway so he could direct the first responders where to go. He rested his hands on his knees trying to catch his breath. Running was not something he was used to doing.

Then he waited.

Megan stayed with Rudy, urging him, willing him, to hang in there until help arrived. She had no idea if he could hear her, but she kept talking to him, reassuring him that help was on the way.

A sheriff's vehicle was the first to arrive. Tony waved it in, then ran ahead to direct it to the boat house. The deputy jumped out of his vehicle, leaving the red and blue lights flashing so the ambulance could easily see where to go.

Tony took the key from behind the sun and moon placque and unlocked the door so they could go directly into the ballroom. Like Megan, the deputy quickly recognized that it was best to not move the injured man. It appeared that he might have broken his neck.

The EMTs arrived a few minutes later.

Once the first responders had taken control of the situation, Tony and Megan stepped outside so they'd be out of the way. They'd done all they could do.

"What happened?" said a woman's voice behind them.

Megan and Tony turned and were surprised to see a familiar face.

"Byrdie!?" said Megan. "What are you doing here?"

"We live here, in the cabin," she said. "This is my partner, Thomas."

"It's Rudy," Megan said. "We found him lying on the stage. He had a bad fall."

"I'm so sorry," said Thomas. "He was such a nice man. We loved him dearly."

"He's not dead," said Tony. "We found him in time."

"Oh, thank God," said Byrdie, exchanging a quick look with the man next to her. "We're so glad that you found him. Will he be okay?"

"Too soon to know," said Megan.

"My real name, by the way, is Sarah," said Byrdie.

"This is my partner, Thomas. We've been helping Rudy take care of the place these past few months."

"We check in on him every day," said Thomas. "We make sure he's eating well and taking his medicine. It's been sad watching him deteriorate so quickly. Some days he doesn't even seem to know where he is. He's really come to depend on us. Calls us his little angels."

They had to get out of the way as the gurney bearing Rudy was wheeled out of the building and into the ambulance.

"We'll be praying for you," said Byrdie, blowing a kiss in the old man's direction.

As the emergency vehicles disappeared from sight, Byrdie looked at Thomas, wiped a tear from her eye, and reassured him that things would be okay.

"We should probably lock up," suggested Byrdie. "It could be awhile before Rudy gets back. Would you two lock up here? Thomas and I will take care of things at the lodge."

"Sure thing," said Megan. "We'll see you up there when we're done."

Tony and Megan went back inside the dance hall. Megan contemplated cleaning up the blood, but realized she didn't have access to any cleaning supplies. That unpleasant task would have to wait for another day. Maybe Byrdie would take care of it.

Megan picked up Rudy's cane and leaned it against the side of the stage before leaving the ballroom through the upper door. Tony took the stairs behind the stage so he could switch off the lights inside the tunnel and close the doors behind himself as he left the boat house.

Before going back to the lodge, Tony locked the upper door and hid the key back under the sculpted sun and moon.

This had not turned out to be the surprise he'd anticipated when he offered to show Megan the ballroom.

They didn't say a word as they walked back to the lodge, but they held each other's hands a little tighter than usual. It was hard to believe that only half an hour earlier they were strolling along this very same lakefront path, commenting how peaceful it was.

Tranquility can be misleading, thought Megan.

Back at the lodge, they did a scan of the deceptively peaceful surroundings before stepping onto the porch.

"We need to remember to take these," Tony said, noticing the pictures and books that they'd left on the porch.

Byrdie was in the kitchen, the top half of an old Oster blender in her hands, the remains of Rudy's morning smoothie dried inside it. She filled it with water to soak.

"That was nice of your friend Martha to leave the bag of greens for Rudy," she said, tossing the mostly empty Ziploc bag in the trash can. "He certainly loves his first-thing-in-the-morning smoothies."

Tony stepped out of the kitchen into the hallway.

"Come look at this," he called from the end of the hall. The others joined him near the small stairway that led up to the maids' rooms. A door at the bottom of the stairs was partially open. It looked like it should be a closet.

"This must be the other end of the tunnel," Tony said. He flipped an old porcelain light switch just inside the door. Several bare bulbs, covered with webs and dirt, illuminated the way down the tunnel.

"Looks like the other end of the 'Thriller' set," Megan said. Only Tony understood what she was referring to.

"This must be how Rudy got down to the boathouse," Byrdie guessed.

"But why?" Tony asked. "He said he never uses this tunnel."

"Someone did," Megan said. She pointed to some dirt and bits of old spider webs stuck to the floor. "Someone came up through this tunnel before Rudy went down. He must have seen their tracks and decided to investigate."

"Do you suppose the exertion of walking through the tunnel wore him out, and that's why he fell when he got to the boathouse?" Byrdie asked.

"He could have been overcome by toxins from the mold in here," Megan said. "The TV renovation shows are always warning us about that."

"Or," said Tony, "the person Rudy was following was at the other end and pushed him."

"This is going from creepy to scary," said Byrdie.

"At least we know they're not there now," Megan said.. "Based on the dried blood where Rudy fell, they've been gone for quite some time."

"Which means," Byrdie said, "whoever pushed him, left him to die."

Tony was about to turn off the lights, when Byrdie grabbed his hand.

"What's that?" she said, pointing to something in the corner, just inside the door.

Tony reached down and picked up a cigarette butt. Unlike everything else in the space, it was not covered with dust and grime.

He paused a moment, then dropped it back onto the floor and pushed it into the corner with his toe.

"It's nothing," he said. "Just more litter. The chipmunk must have dragged it in here."

He flipped off the lights and closed the door, then slid his hand along the upper sill and found the key.

"The door must not have been locked," he said, pointing out that the key was coated with dust. He turned the key in the lock, jiggled the handle to make sure it was latched, then put the key back where he'd found it.

"You two do a walk through upstairs," Byrdie instructed. "Thomas and I can finish down here."

When Tony and Megan came back downstairs, the young couple was in Rudy's room. Byrdie was flipping through some folders in his filing cabinet.

"What are you doing?" Megan asked.

"I figured we'd better find Rudy's health insurance stuff and take it over to the hospital," she said, pulling out a couple of file folders. The one on top had the words Health Insurance written boldly in Sharpie on the front. She handed it to Thomas.

"Oh dear," she said softly as she looked at the next folder. It was labelled Last Will and Testament. "Let's hope we won't need this," she said putting it back in the drawer. "But at least we know where it is."

"I guess we've got everything that we need, then," Thomas said. He turned to Tony and Megan. "Everything as it should be upstairs?"

"Looks okay up there," said Tony.

"Do you suppose we should be notifying anyone?" Megan asked.

"I don't know who we'd notify," said Byrdie. "Rudy has no family, other than us. And we're not actual family, he just treats us that way."

"We'll take this to the hospital," Thomas said, holding up the insurance folder.

"Thank you for your help," Byrdie said once they were all out on the porch and she had locked the door. "It was such a blessing that you found Rudy when you did."

"Let us know how he's doing," Megan called to the young couple as they walked back to their cabin.

"Will do," Byrdie said with a wave.

"I didn't realize how bad of shape Rudy was in," said Tony as they drove out the driveway. "The feeble old man that they described doesn't match at all with the Rudy that you and I met."

"We barely know him. They care for him every day."

"That's another thing. Rudy gave me the impression that they stop by every couple of days, just to say hi."

"Maybe he was too proud to admit to you that he needs full-time caregivers."

Tony just shrugged.

They stopped at the hospital on the way back to Blackbird Cabin to see if they could learn anything about Rudy's condition. They were told he was still in the ER and there was nothing more they could tell them, especially since they weren't family.

They decided they would check again the next day. Hopefully, they'd hear something from Byrdie.

"Do you think we should return his books to the library?" Tony asked as they pulled out of the hospital parking lot.

Megan gave him a look that made him wish he hadn't even suggested it.

"Like you said at the boathouse, 'he's not dead'! Let's stay positive. We'll hang onto the books and give them to him when he's feeling up to reading."

Chapter 18

"I'm surprised we haven't heard anything from Byrdie about how Rudy is doing," said Megan late the next morning.

She thought a moment, then asked Tony: "Did you give her your number? I didn't give her mine."

"No. I guess that would explain why we haven't heard from her."

"I'm not sure that she even knows our names other than Moonflower and Moon Dog. We're still calling her Byrdie."

"True. I have no idea how we'd contact her, either, other than going over to their cabin."

"After lunch, let's go to the hospital," Megan suggested. "We could bring him some flowers."

"I've still got the foxglove bouquet that Mr. Bones was holding. It's held up pretty well. Do you suppose he'd like that? Something to remind him of home?"

"Not sure that reminding him of home would be the best thing right now. We can stop on the way and pick up something fresh."

"Pretty nice hospital for a small town," Tony commented as they stepped into the bright and cheerful lobby. It was the first time they'd been there.

"We're here to see Rudy Rogers," said Tony.

They were given his room number and headed off to see him. Megan was carrying a small vase of daisies.

When they reached the room, they heard voices through the partially closed door.

"That's a good sign," Tony said softly. "I'll bet it's Byrdie and Thomas."

He knocked gently on the door. The voices inside stopped and they could hear someone walking toward them.

A woman opened the door.

It wasn't Byrdie.

"Hello," she said, reaching out and giving Megan a hug. "I'm so glad that you came."

"Martha, we didn't expect to see you here," said Megan. "How is Rudy doing?"

"Come in and see for yourself."

Rudy, as they expected, was in a hospital bed and had an IV attached to his arm. He was also hooked up to a monitor, its wavy lines and blips telling a story to those who knew how to interpret them. The area around his eyes was black and blue, like he'd lost a fight to the school bully. Attached to his head was a brace holding his neck in place.

Megan held up the flowers so Rudy could see them. He moved his eyes toward them and blinked, acknowledging their presence. She set the bouquet on the dresser within his field of vision.

"I had something that I needed Rudy to see," Martha

said, answering the unspoken question of why she was there. "I drove out to the lodge this morning to show it to him, but everything was locked up tight. I heard an engine running and went toward the sound, expecting to find Rudy mowing the lawn. Much to my surprise it was Byrdie from the mystery dinner. I didn't realize that she lived in the cabin right there at Foxglove Lodge.

"Anyway, Byrdie explained to me what had happened."

She leaned forward and gave Megan a hug.

"It was a stroke of providence that the two of you came along when you did. The doctors said that a few more hours alone and he'd have been gone."

"What's the prognosis?" asked Megan.

"As you can probably guess, his neck was injured in the fall. They don't want him moving it at all for a few days. Also, his jaw is fractured. They wired it shut, so he can't talk or eat."

Megan reached over and took the man's hand. It felt cold.

"They're not sure what caused him to fall," Martha continued. "It may have been a heart issue. His heartbeat was irregular when they found him, but that's improved."

"Could it have been related to his heart meds?" Megan asked.

"Possibly. Too much time had passed between when he'd last taken his pills—he uses one of those little pill containers marked for each day of the week—and the time he arrived here. It's impossible to tell what his levels were when he fell."

Rudy's eyes slowly moved back and forth between his guests. It seemed like he wanted to be part of the conversation, if only he could.

"I thought we heard people talking when we were at the door," said Tony.

"Oh, that." Martha pointed to a laptop on the tray across Rudy's bed. "We were watching some old music documentaries on YouTube. He can move his fingers okay on the touch pad to navigate to the clips that he wants."

It wasn't the laptop that his fingers were on now. He squeezed the button to self administer a dose of pain killer.

"We'd better be going," Tony said to Megan.

"Rudy, you hang in there," Megan said. "We'll come back and see you again."

Rudy gently closed his eyes, the pain killer taking effect.

Martha walked out to the hall with them.

"He looks pretty rough," Megan said softly.

Martha acknowledged the obvious. "He's so doped up that I'm not sure he knows what's going on. When he's lucid, he seems frustrated that he's unable to tell us anything about what happened."

"I'm glad that you were here to fill us in," said Megan as they were ready to leave. "The nurses wouldn't tell us anything because we weren't family. What trick did you use to convince them to tell you?"

She put her finger to her lips.

"I told them I was his daughter."

Chapter 19

Tony and Megan decided to take a little trip to get away from it all.

For most folks, 'getting away from it all' meant heading up to the Northwoods. For Megan and Tony, it meant taking a drive farther north to Copper Harbor, at the tip of the Keweenaw peninsula, the farthest point north in Michigan's Upper Peninsula.

Even though they had their own lake view at Blackbird Cabin, it didn't compare to gazing out over Lake Superior, watching huge, oceangoing freighters making their way across the endless horizon.

They were thrilled to find a room at the Copper Queen motel, a little place overlooking the harbor. The single-story motel hadn't changed much in the decades it'd been there.

Parking was along one side of a long row of windowless doors. On the opposite side of the building, patio doors from each room opened onto a park-like area with benches and picnic tables. Just across the street, which catered more to walkers than vehicles, was a small coffee shop that sold freshly made bakery until it was gone. It was also a fish market. And offered a few shirts and hats.

During the warm months, the idyllic harbor town bustled with a gentle breed of tourists. There were no chain restaurants or motels in this community of about a hundred and fifty souls. Everything was locally owned and operated.

One of the highlights for Tony and Megan was playing eighteen holes at the tiny mini-golf course on the edge of town. It appeared to have been built by someone in their side yard. Nothing too fancy, but the fee was right and one never had to worry about someone wanting to play through. It was a completely self-serve operation.

They dropped their money into a small slot on the door of the clubhouse (which was also a storage shed), selected their clubs and balls and played away. When done, they put everything back where they found it. As usual, they dutifully noted their number of strokes on the score card, but didn't bother to add it up at the end.

"It feels good to be away from the hustle and bustle of the big city," joked Megan as they relaxed in the lawn chairs outside their motel room.

Their Northwoods 'big city' had less than nine thousand residents, which, compared to Copper Harbor, was pretty darn big.

Mostly, it felt good to be away from the craziness of the last couple of weeks, what with the murder mystery dinner, the theft of Rudy's guitar and the discovery of his body draped over the edge of the stage in the ballroom.

That evening they strolled down to the Harbor View restaurant, which featured fresh-caught Lake Superior fish and traditional Bavarian cuisine. The entire wall of the second-floor dining area was glass, providing a spectacular view of the Isle Royale ferry setting out on its sunset cruise.

When they'd finished eating, they drove up to the top of Brockway Mountain, which overlooked the village, and joined several other tourists in watching the sun disappear over the vast expanse of water. It was amazing how much faster the sun went down over the water than it did through the trees.

The next morning they walked across the street to the coffee shop in time to get a still-warm sweet roll, which they enjoyed on a concrete park bench situated a few feet from the rocky shore.

"I'm glad that we came up here," said Megan.

"Me too," said Tony. "How about we take the long way home, along the other side of the peninsula?"

"That's fine with me. I'm in no rush."

After leaving their room key, an actual key, not a key card, at the office they headed out. They took their time, stopping at a cute little rock shop that specialized in agates and jewelry made from local copper. It was as much a museum as it was a store.

Lunch was a sub sandwich eaten on the rocks at Eagle Harbor Lighthouse, a historical site a few miles down the road from the rock shop. They considered touring the lighthouse, but decided against it. They were enjoying their day alone and didn't feel like being part of a tour group.

After lunch they picked the road that seemed to run closest to the shore, sometimes following small loops that were little more than public access driveways leading to lakeside cottages not much bigger than their own.

At one point they pulled into a parking area that was immediately adjacent to a long expanse of shoreline. The beach there was covered with millions of small rocks and random pieces of driftwood. Several rock collectors wandered the beach, eyes down, hoping to find the perfect gem for their collection or next art project

Tony and Megan simply strolled along the waterline, avoiding the surf each time it came up to greet them.

Halfway home they discovered an antique store in an old bank. They had the place to themselves. It was so filled with treasures and odds and ends that it was difficult to get through the aisles. Tony found a couple of interesting books and Megan discovered a doll from her childhood, but they weren't sure who to buy them from. A sign at the check-out counter said that they should pay across the street at what appeared to be a competing antique store.

"You've gotta love the way people trust each other in these small towns," Megan said. "Nice place."

The sun was just about down by the time they pulled up to Blackbird Cabin. An owl hooted a greeting, not to them but to another owl that answered.

What a perfect way to end a wonderfully relaxing day, thought Tony as he unlocked the cabin door.

Megan's phone rang.

It was Martha.

Rudy was dead.

Chapter 20

"I'm going to work on the trail," Tony said to Megan the next morning, chain saw in one hand, axe in the other.

Busywork, physical work, seemed like a good way to take his mind off of Rudy's death and the events leading up to it. It was difficult to keep his brain from running nonstop scenarios that included the words woulda, coulda, and shoulda.

Martha hadn't provided any details about Rudy's death. Apparently his broken heart just finally gave out. Tony figured that the trauma from his fall, along with the stress from his guitar being stolen, were probably contributing factors.

Megan noticed the stack of books sitting on the table, right where she'd set them three days ago. Obviously, Rudy wasn't going to be up to reading them. The photographs that Tony had taken of Rudy were there, too.

"We need to take these books back to the library," she said matter-of-factly when her tired and sweaty husband came in for lunch. "What do you plan to do about the brochure? The art fair is tomorrow."

"I'll stop at their booth and explain that I couldn't get them done, but I can't imagine they're expecting them.

Besides, it seems almost creepy now to have Rudy's smiling face on a brochure encouraging people to leave their money to the library after they're gone."

Megan looked out the window where several blackbirds had congregated.

If Rudy hadn't agreed to help with the library's fund raiser, he might still be with us, she thought. *On the other hand, if he hadn't offered the use of his lodge, Tony and I wouldn't have even met him.*

It was as if getting to know him was nothing more than a cruel tease, his potential friendship yanked away as soon as they showed any interest.

After a quiet lunch, Tony decided to head back to the woods rather than go to the library with Megan.

"Would you drop the pictures off when you return the books?" he asked.

"Sure," she said. "Be safe."

"Quite a shock about Rudy," the librarian said as Megan handed him the books. "I'll miss my Tuesday visits with him."

"I wish I'd have had a chance to get to know him better," she said. "He seemed like a nice guy."

"He was."

The librarian looked puzzled as he checked the books back in.

"This is odd," he said as much to himself as to Megan.

"What is?"

"Rudy has four more books on the hold shelf. He reserved them yesterday."

"A reader 'til the end," observed Megan. "Just out of

curiosity, what are the books?"

"I guess it won't hurt to tell you," he said. "More murder mysteries. The guy knew what he liked, that's for sure. I'll return them to the shelf. They're all from our collection."

As the librarian removed the books from the hold shelf, Megan snuck a peek at the titles:

- *Appointment With Death*, Agatha Christie
- *Postern of Fate*, Agatha Christie
- *The Herb of Death*, Agatha Christie
- *Crooked House*, Agatha Christie

Megan wasn't sure why, but she jotted down the titles as soon as she got back in the car. As she shifted into reverse, she noticed the envelope containing the pictures of Rudy. It had slipped down between the seat and the console. She considered going back inside, then decided that the pictures were fine right where they were.

When she got home, Tony was grumpy. He'd pinched his chain saw while removing a widow maker. In the process of trying to force it free, he not only broke the chain but bent the bar. He didn't have a spare.

Without knowing what had transpired in the woods, Megan told him that she'd forgotten to leave the pictures at the library.

"I can't imagine they would be of much use now, anyway," he grumbled. "Sorry. But thanks for taking them along."

"Something interesting came up at the library," Megan said.

"What's that?"

"It looks like Rudy's death must have been as much of a surprise to him as it was to the rest of us. Just yesterday, he put a bunch of library books on hold."

She pulled out the list of titles and handed it to Tony. "Take a look."

"This must be a mistake," he said. "These are all Agatha Christie mysteries. Rudy has every one of these stories in his personal library. Could someone else have mistakenly reserved them in his name?"

"It's possible, I suppose. If they had his card and password they could reserve them online. But why would someone do that?"

Tony shrugged his shoulders and stuck the list in his wallet.

Chapter 21

The crowd at the art fair was enthusiastic and filled with positive energy. This was Tony's first time at an art fair as a seller. He and Megan had meandered through a number of similar events in the past, browsing, buying, and getting ideas for their own projects, but sitting behind a little, fabric-draped table with a cash box would be an entirely different experience.

After he'd set up his table he walked over to the Friends of the Library's booth and explained that he didn't have the brochures. They hadn't been expecting them. He enjoyed looking at the scale model of the proposed library expansion that they had on display. Seeing that model made the project feel real.

"Is Martha going to be here?" he asked. "I had a question for her."

"She was supposed to be here to help us set up. Not sure where she is."

Tony returned to his table, ready for the fair's opening. He was the only vendor selling books and being surrounded by 'real' artists selling their paintings, wood carvings, hand-made jewelry and yard art, he was worried about fitting in.

It didn't take long before he had his first customer and was pleasantly surprised at how well he was being received.

He enjoyed chatting with the locals who'd already read his novel, many of whom had recognized the various 'fictionalized' settings he'd included in the story. A number of them wanted to tell him tales that their own families had passed along from long ago in the Northwoods.

He was especially surprised by the number of people who asked if he'd mind signing their copy of the book. Mind? He was honored. A couple of buyers even took their pictures with him.

Megan joined him at lunch time so he could get a break and find something to eat.

"How are things going?" she asked. "Selling any books?"

"I've already sold seven," he said.

"Good job. And the day's only half over."

"Did you stop at the library booth?"

"I did. I was surprised that Martha wasn't there. I wanted to ask if she knew if there was some kind of memorial being planned for Rudy. It seems like she's become the contact person for info about him since his fall."

When Tony returned about fifteen minutes later, Megan said: "I made another sale while you were away and I have a suggestion. People would appreciate it if you had bags to put their books in, rather than smudging up the cover with their sweaty hands on such a warm day."

"Good idea. I hadn't thought of that."

"Looks like business is good," said a familiar voice. It

was Kenny, the director of the local historical museum. He'd helped Tony answer some questions about area history when he was writing his novel.

"Can't complain," Tony responded. "I'm not used to sitting here and being friendly for this long at a stretch, but it's fun talking with people about my story. And even more fun listening to their stories."

"My kind of people," Kenny smiled. "Are you working on anything new?"

"Not exactly. You may have heard that I put together the script for the library's murder mystery dinner. Unfortunately, that didn't quite turn out so good."

"Yes. Bummer about the guitar," said Kenny, who was also a musician. "But from what I've heard, the people at the dinner had a fun evening."

"Glad to hear that," Tony responded. "We haven't heard from anyone who was there."

"But" Megan interjected, "aside from one young lady who we recently met, we don't actually know the real-life identities of any of the folks who were there."

"I was shocked to learn about Rudy," said Kenny. "It was only about a month ago that he invited me out to the lodge to talk about leaving the resort to the museum. He thought we could run it as a living history site."

"Not to sound crass," said Megan, "but I suppose you're looking forward to his will being read."

Kenny slowly shook his head, as if to say *Rudy, Rudy, Rudy, what were you thinking?* "I don't believe he had any idea how hard it would be for a small organization like ours to take on such a huge project without some serious, long-term planning. It was a very generous offer, to be sure, and it would be a great way to preserve some Northwoods history, but we simply aren't ready to take it on today.

"I've heard that there's going to be a celebration of life for Rudy next Saturday," Kenny continued, "and that I should plan to be there. As I understand it, that's when the will is going to be read. To be honest, I'm kinda hoping that he hadn't yet gotten around to including us, or, if he did, that he included provisions for some sort of ongoing support."

"I guess you'll find out next weekend. Do you have any details about the memorial?"

"Nope. Someone left a message asking me to be at the lodge on Saturday afternoon."

"That's all we know, too," said Megan.

She looked at Tony. "I'm going to stop over at the Friends table and then check out some of the art," she interjected. "Nice seeing you, Kenny. Tony, I'll see you at home."

"Thanks for the break," he said, then gave his wife a quick kiss goodbye.

"Any word on what happened to Rudy's guitar?" Kenny asked after Megan was gone. "That's quite a loss."

"Nothing yet."

"Since the guitar's got historical significance, I put the word out to my friends at other museums, in case someone inquiries about the value of such an instrument. I doubt if I'll hear anything, but it doesn't hurt to let people know. The more folks on the lookout for the guitar, the better our chances of getting it back to ...."

He started over. "The better our chance of finding the

person who stole it so they can be held responsible. It's the least we can do for the old guy. That guitar really meant the world to him."

"Did he tell you about using it when he wrote 'The Tunnel of Love?'"

"He did. Pretty cool to discover the local link to that song. He even showed me the tunnel."

"Did he take you through it?"

"No, he said it was so dirty and full of spider webs that it was impassable. But we did get to talking about secret tunnels in the area. His was originally built during prohibition to sneak booze into the resort. It could be delivered by boat at night and brought into the lodge without anyone ever seeing. It also worked well for discreetly ferrying bottles of liquor from the lodge to the club house across the bay. After prohibition, the tunnel was a handy way for the resort staff to bring food and beverages to the ballroom."

"And for the staff to sneak musicians up to their rooms," Tony laughed. "Ah, to be young and foolish."

As Kenny said his farewell, a woman with a copy of "The Secret of Blackbird Cabin" asked Tony if he'd mind signing it.

He pulled out his Sharpie.

"I'd be honored."

Chapter 22

"The art fair turned out better than I expected," Tony said as he brought the folding table and half-empty box of books back into the cabin. "Thank you for coming by and giving me a break."

"Glad to help. How many did you end up selling?"

"Enough to pay for the booth fee and cover some of my printing costs. Plus, I met some very interesting people."

"Glad that it went well. I was proud seeing my 'famous' husband sitting there signing autographs. I kept an eye on you as I wandered around other parts of the fair. Was it my imagination or does it seem like your biggest fans are older women?"

"They're the only ones with time to read a book," he laughed. "Speaking of older women, have you heard anything from Martha today? Before I left the square, I asked the folks from the Friends group about her and they said she never did show up."

"That's odd. From the limited time I've spent with her, she's been very responsible. Maybe she needed to take a break, like our escape to Copper Harbor."

"Could be."

"I hope you're hungry," she said, holding up a bag from

the grocery store. "To celebrate your successful day at the art fair, I picked up some cranberry brats and those bakery buns that you like. I even found you a bock beer. It looks like a perfect evening to start up the grill. I've got a new crop of mushrooms, too, that we could sauté with butter."

By the next afternoon, the couple still hadn't heard anything from Martha and she didn't answer or respond when Megan called her. They decided to drive out to Foxglove Lodge to see if Byrdie might have any details about the memorial on Saturday.

They drove past the lodge and stopped at the little cabin with the flower boxes. Tony knocked on the door, but no one seemed to be around.

"Let's check at the lodge," Megan said. "Maybe they're working up there."

"I wonder where they'll go after the estate is closed?" Tony said as they walked along the lakeshore to the lodge. "It sounded like they had more or less a handshake agreement with Rudy to live here."

"Isn't that Martha's car?" Megan asked, noticing a vehicle parked along the back side of the lodge, hidden under the trees.

They went up onto the porch. The front door was open and they could hear someone inside.

Tony and Megan stepped into the Great Hall. The sound was coming from Rudy's room. They quietly walked down the hall and looked in. A woman, her back toward them, was rummaging through Rudy's dresser, piling things into a suitcase.

"What's going on?" asked Megan.

The startled intruder turned and discreetly closed the suitcase. On the floor next to her was a banker's box, filled with various pieces of Rudy's musical memorabilia.

"Martha," Megan said. "We've been trying to get hold of you."

"Oh, hi, sorry," she said, fumbling blindly with the latch on the suitcase. "I've been trying to get some things ready for the celebration of Rudy's life on Saturday. I hope you can be there."

"We plan to, but we don't know much about what's going on. Are you in charge of it?"

"Seems that way. No one else stepped up."

"How about the young couple from the cabin? Are they helping you?" asked Tony.

"Not really. They brought the insurance info to the hospital and said they gave the will to the lawyer, but other than that, I haven't heard a word from them."

"Will there be a visitation at the funeral home?" Megan asked.

"No. Just the celebration on Saturday with the disposition of ashes."

Megan glanced at Tony. They both had the same question. "If there's no visitation," Megan asked, "why are you collecting Rudy's clothes?"

"It doesn't seem very respectful to have someone cremated wrapped in a sheet, does it," she stammered. "A person deserves better, don't you think?"

Martha looked down at the box on the floor, anticipating the couple's next question.

"Those are things I thought could be displayed around

the urn on Saturday. They help tell Rudy's story."

At the top of the pile was the framed, autographed picture of Rudy and the Rockets.

"That picture says it all, doesn't it?" said Martha. "It will be front and center. Too bad we don't have his guitar to display."

"Is there anything else we can do to help?" asked Tony, still feeling bad about the valuable guitar being stolen during their watch.

"You could spread the word about Saturday. It's too late to get it in the paper."

"Do you think the participants from the mystery dinner would be interested in showing their respects?" Megan asked. "They were the last people to enjoy his generosity."

"I think that would be great. If you could let them know, it'd be appreciated. The library should have their contact info."

"Do we need to bring anything?"

Martha thought for a moment, then asked, almost timidly: "Do you have an old boom box that plays cassettes?"

Tony said that he still had one that he used out in the barn when he was working.

"Could you bring it along?" she asked. "I'd like to scatter the ashes from the boathouse balcony and I think it'd be fitting if we could have Rudy's music playing in the background. I found a cassette at Goodwill with 'Tunnel of Love' on it."

"That seems like a perfect send off," said Tony. "I'll be sure to bring it with us."

Chapter 23

On the way back from Foxglove Lodge, they stopped at the library. While Megan secured the list of dinner participants, Tony pulled out the list of titles that Rudy had placed on hold. All four of the Agatha Christie stories were back on the shelf. He decided to check them out.

"Why'd you get those?" Megan asked when they were back in the car.

"I can't help but wonder why he put them on hold. Something doesn't seem right. He already had his own copies of each of them. Maybe he was trying to send a message to someone at the library."

Tony spent the rest of the day in his favorite lakeside chair, speed reading through the novels he'd brought from the library.

"Finding anything interesting?" Megan asked when he finally decided it was time to come in.

"As a matter of fact, *mon ami*," he grinned, twirling his non-existent mustaches, "my little grey cells have been working overtime. I have discovered something most intriguing."

"And what might that be, my little Belgium friend?"

"These stories, they have something in common," he

explained, continuing to channel Miss Christie's favorite detective. "In each one, the victim was poisoned with digitalis. With foxglove."

"That woman liked her poison, didn't she."

"It gets better," he said, back in his normal voice. "In one story, foxglove leaves were mixed with salad greens and served at a dinner party."

"We served mixed salad greens at our mystery dinner."

"Exactly. When you first told me what was on your menu, I decided to add a clue in my script about foxglove plants, leading—or misleading—our sleuths in that direction."

"Good thing that no one got poisoned that night," she smiled, "or you'd be a suspect in their murders."

"Of course, I didn't *really* put foxglove leaves in the salad greens. It was just a clue, for the game. A clue which no one actually noticed, anyway, so it made no difference."

"Is that what finding the cigarette butt in the flower bed was all about?"

"Yes, it was supposed to be a clue as to who had picked the foxglove leaves."

"I've been wondering about something. The game didn't end up the way that you planned, did it? According to your script, who was the murderer supposed to be?"

"It was supposed to be Byrdie, with Janis's help in gathering the foxglove leaves. That's why I linked Byrdie to the empty prescription bottle and dropped Janis's cigarette butt next to the foxglove plants."

"Good job of letting the participants solve the mystery spontaneously on their own, instead of forcing your ending on them. It all worked out quite well."

"Thank you. But I have to give much of the credit to Byrdie for her marvelous denouement. She was quite the little actress. I think she recognized that a number of the clues were pointing in her direction and decided to turn the tables and make everyone believe that someone else was the murderer."

"That's interesting, but how does it relate to Rudy and the books he placed on hold? He wasn't even in town during the murder mystery dinner."

"I'm still working on that. I know that Rudy was taking digitalis for his heart condition. But since he wasn't at the mystery dinner, he didn't eat any of the greens."

"That's not exactly true," Megan pointed out. "He *did* eat the greens, just not at the dinner. Martha suggested that we bag up the extras and leave them in the refrigerator for him."

"Do we know if he ate them?"

"When we closed up the lodge, after you and I found him in the boathouse, I noticed the empty Ziploc bag on the kitchen counter. There were still a few leaves stuck to the inside. And I recall that Byrdie was washing out the blender—she was scrubbing hard because it was so dried on. Rudy must have used the greens to make himself a smoothie a day or two earlier. Since no one at the murder mystery got sick, the poisonous leaves must have been added to the bag after the dinner."

"Not necessarily," Tony said. "I never finished telling you Agatha's story. The key to that puzzle was that the foxglove leaves had been mixed into *everyone's* salads, but most dinner guests were not poisoned because of the small amount they ingested. Only one person died, because the murderer knew that his target was already taking digitalis for a heart condition and that the additional toxin from the greens would cause an overdose."

"Now that I think about it," Megan said slowly, "the salads that Martha served were pretty tiny."

Megan decided it was her turn to pose a solution.

"How about this: The murderer was anticipating that Rudy would be hosting the dinner. But when he was a no show, his plan fell apart. Thinking on the fly, the greens were left for Rudy to use to make his daily smoothie."

"You said that Martha bagged up the greens. Do we know who provided them for the dinner?"

"I'm not sure. Martha said that the greens came from Rudy's garden, but I don't know who picked them. He might have picked them himself and left them for the party."

"Ok, here's another idea," said Tony.

They were on a roll.

"Rudy offered to host the murder mystery dinner at his lodge because *he* was planning to murder one of the people who would be attending. We know Rudy was a huge fan of murder mystery novels. Maybe he wanted to create his own Agatha Christie-style mystery using the dinner as his cover. He planned to set up an actual murder that he could then solve. Like the arsonist who is also a fire fighter."

"One major flaw in that scenario: Why would he solve a murder that he committed?"

"Because he'd solve it incorrectly, just like Byrdie did, deflecting blame from himself. Rudy was planning to commit the perfect murder!"

"Go on..."

"Picture this: Rudy gathers the suspects together in the Great Hall. Once he has everyone's attention, he dramatically and methodically weaves his tale and finally reveals who had committed the crime. Here's the twist. The person he accuses of the crime is the person that he originally intended to kill. Problem solved. He'd be recognized as a genius crime solver. By exposing someone else as the killer, he would have committed the perfect crime. No one would even suspect him, because he was conveniently far away at a concert."

"Quite the dramatic scenario, but you do realize that there's a couple of gigantic holes in your plot."

"Such as?"

"First, if he was at a concert, how could he be at the lodge solving the crime?"

"Good point."

"Second, no one actually died at the mystery dinner. There was no murder for him to solve."

Tony thought for a moment.

"Okay, the murder he needed to solve was ... his own!"

"You've got my attention."

"Imagine this: Rudy accidently falls and hits his head in the boathouse."

"Which did actually happen."

"While he's lying there, falling in and out of consciousness, he recognizes that he has one last chance to not only commit the perfect crime, but to also demonstrate his brilliance as a detective."

"Are you saying Rudy actually wanted to kill someone?"

"Seems unlikely, doesn't it, but I'm on a roll here. For the sake of my story, let's suppose that Rudy did have someone he wanted to kill. Unfortunately, since he was sprawled out on the floor unable to move, he was in no position—pun intended—to do that. But he could still frame someone for murdering him! Quite brilliant, really."

Megan just shook her head. "I think you're the one who's hit his head too hard. How does any of this tie in to the reality of Rudy putting those four books on reserve at the library?"

"Simple. He was stuck in the hospital unable to accuse anyone of his murder. He couldn't speak. He was too weak to write out his accusation or even send it as an email. So he came up with another way to tell us what happened, using his laptop which Martha had brought in. He had only enough energy to hit the few keystrokes it'd take to put those four books on hold. He'd let Agatha explain how he was murdered. With only a few taps on the keyboard, he was able to get the incriminating books onto the hold shelf, where he knew someone would find them after he died. He probably used the last of his energy to hit send. Rudy left us a message from the grave."

"I'm not so sure I like his message," Megan said. "I'd rather remember him as a sweet old man with a broken heart, not someone who was plotting to show off his detective skills by planning the perfect murder."

"That still leaves one important question," said Tony. "Who did Rudy want dead?"

"And why?" added Megan.

Chapter 24

"That was a pretty weird crime-storming session we had last night," Megan said as she and Tony were eating their breakfast.

"It was."

"Does it feel to you like we're creating mysteries where none really exist? That we're so into playing detective that we're forgetting this isn't a game?"

"At least we didn't create a Board of Clues this time," Tony laughed.

"That's only because I used all the string tying up the plants in the garden. Speaking of gardens, so far so good on the foxglove plants. The jury's still out on the yarrow and snap dragons. A couple of them seem to be shorter now than when I planted them."

As they were putting away their breakfast dishes, Tony said: "Maybe we're wasting our time trying to prove that something sinister happened to Rudy, but I can't stop worrying that he was trying to send a message by putting those books on hold and if we don't figure out what it was, no one will."

"I know how you feel. I've been trying to convince myself that he put those books on hold because he believed he'd soon be out of the hospital and was looking forward to another of his Tuesday morning visits to the library."

"I like that theory. Puts a nice, positive spin on the situation."

"You're not really buying it, though, are you?"

"Not really."

"Me neither."

Tony went out to the barn to get the boom box. He returned a few minutes later. The once-stylish music machine was filthy from its many years of being used outdoors and in the workshop. He cleaned it off and plugged it in. The radio still worked.

He pushed the buttons on the cassette player. The little wheels went around, but without a cassette there was no way to determine if any sound would come out.

"Megan, do you know where Martha lives?"

"Not specifically. I think it's a little ways out of town, just past the nursery. Why?"

"I need to test this out before Saturday. She has the Rudy and the Rockets cassette that I'm planning to play. I'd like to try it out to make sure it'll work. The last thing we need is to hit play in Rudy's memory and the machine starts making horrible sounds as the tape is being devoured."

"Yea, that probably wouldn't be the greatest send off. I'll give her a call and see where she lives."

"That was odd," Megan said a few minutes later. "I got her address, but she seemed rather hesitant about us coming over. She said she didn't want to inconvenience us and would bring the cassette along on Saturday."

"That won't work. I need to test it out before then. It'd

be more of an inconvenience to have to wait."

"I suppose we could just drive over and pick it up."

"It sure is pretty back here," Megan commented as they turned onto the tree-canopied township road where Martha lived. "Hard to believe we're so close to town. It feels like you're way out in the woods."

"This must be the place," Tony said, checking the fire number beside the mailbox. There were no other houses nearby. He pulled into the gravel driveway and stopped in front of a cute little bungalow that looked like it had been here for quite some time. A TV antenna atop a tall wooden pole stood watch next to the house. A long wooden ramp went up to the front porch. Before they could even get out of the car, Martha appeared on the porch.

"Hi," she said. "I hadn't expected you."

"I thought it'd be best to try out the boom box before Saturday," said Tony, getting out of the car.

"Cute place, you've got here," Megan said, stepping into the yard. "You said that your mom lived here?"

"Yes," Martha said, without leaving the porch. "I grew up in this house. I moved away after high school and took a job in Milwaukee, but when Mom's health started going downhill, I took early retirement and moved back to help her out."

"I'm sure she appreciates that. How is she doing?"

"I'm afraid she passed away last year."

"Oh, I'm sorry to hear that," said Megan, her eyes glancing toward a wheelchair near the front door.

"It's been hard for me to get rid of her things," Martha

said, nodding toward the chair. "I'm planning to donate that to the thrift store. I just haven't gotten around to it. That's why it's sitting there. So I don't forget."

"We could take it with us, if that would be helpful," Tony offered. "The thrift store isn't out of our way."

"Thanks, but I don't want to inconvenience you. Let me get you the cassette. Wait here."

She hurried back into the house and quickly returned with the cassette. She handed it to Tony.

"I hope this works," she said. "Thanks for helping out. See you on Saturday."

"Well, that was quick," said Megan as they headed back to Blackbird Cabin. "I kinda expected to get more of a welcome, maybe be shown around the place. She's got some nicely established flower beds I'd like to ask her about."

"Another time," Tony said. "I'm sure she'll be more welcoming once things get back to normal for her."

"And for us."

Tony was relieved to see and hear that the old boom box did not eat the Rudy and the Rockets cassette.

"That sounds pretty good," said Megan after the music ended. "I'm impressed. I even recognized a couple of the tunes. It was fun to hear 'Tunnel of Love.' I don't recall hearing that one before."

"Those guys could rock. I don't think this old boom box will cut it, though, for his send off on Saturday. I'm going to try to connect it to Rudy's old guitar amplifier so we get some decent sounding music in the dance hall."

"Shouldn't it be more subdued for a memorial?"

"Rudy was an old rocker. Subdued wasn't his thing. Their most popular song was called 'Blast Off!'"

"Good point. It does seem that memorials today are more about celebrating a person's life, rather than mourning their passing."

Chapter 25

Tony was excited.

"Are you up for a drive to La Crosse?" he asked Megan as she stepped out of the shower Friday morning.

"Why do we need to go to La Crosse?"

"I got a call from Doug's Guitar Shop. They just got an online request for an appraisal of an instrument that sounds like Rudy's Stratocaster. They asked if I could come down there and help identify it. I was hoping that we could make a day of it."

"That's great news that they found the guitar... I guess. Too bad Rudy's not here to get it back. Why'd they contact you?"

"The guy from the music store here in town had alerted Doug to the loss of Rudy's guitar, with the instructions to contact Rudy if it was found. Obviously, that's no longer an option, so they decided to call me, since Rudy and I had been searching for it together."

"Do you know the guitar well enough to identify it?"

"Probably not. I've only played it once, for a few minutes. But Doug said it would still be helpful if I was there."

"How late are they open?"

"They close at six. But we'd need to get there by four. The guy is scheduled to bring the guitar to the shop at about four thirty. Doug was hoping that I could be there when the guitar is brought in."

"How long does it take to get to La Crosse from here?"

"About four hours. Four and a half if we stop for lunch along the way."

"It's a nice day for a drive," Megan said, considering her options. "Would we have time to stop at that basement antique store in Black River on the way?"

"If we leave soon, that should work. We can eat lunch along the river and then take the scenic route to La Crosse."

"Okay. We might as well make an enjoyable day out of what is, in some ways, a sad situation."

"Thanks. I always enjoy your company."

"You're welcome. But next time, at least let me dry my hair before you ask me out on a date."

After an enjoyable lunch along the river, they went into town to check out the antique store. It was an unusual place, its entrance nearly hidden down a flight of stairs at the back of one of the old downtown businesses. The room filled the full footprint of the business above it, but still felt cozy, probably because of its low ceilings and tiny widows at the top of the walls.

Megan wandered through its various nooks and crannies, on the lookout for vintage dolls, the kind that would have been popular when she was a child.

Tony was thrilled to find a box full of old 45 RPM records priced at one dollar each. He'd never heard of many of the artists, but the ones he did recognize brought back great memories: "Hang on Sloopy" by the McCoys, "I Love You So Much" by the New Colony Six and "Kind of a Drag" by the Buckinghams. As he was almost at the end of the pile, he came across "Blast Off" by Rudy and the Rockets. He quickly flipped it over to the other side and there it was: "Tunnel of Love."

"Megan," he said finding her several aisles away. "Look what I found!"

"Wow! I knew there was a reason we were supposed to stop here on the way to La Crosse."

"This will be perfect to display at the memorial tomorrow. The 'Tunnel of Love' track on the cassette is part of a compilation of classic tunes. This is the real deal! Too bad I can't get Rudy to autograph it."

They pulled up to Doug's Guitar Shop shortly before four. There were only a couple other cars in the lot. After a quick glance around the store, they went upstairs, past Doug's incomparable collection of vintage guitars, and knocked on the door to his office.

"Thank you for coming," Doug said after they'd introduced themselves. "I was sorry to learn of Rudy's passing. He had an early impact on me as a guitarist. That Stratocaster of his is a beautiful instrument. I tried to talk him into selling it to me for my collection, but he wasn't willing to part with it just yet. Said he'd let me know when he was ready."

"He told me that you gave it an upgrade a few years ago," Tony said.

"Not an upgrade. Just a thorough cleaning. We checked

the electronics, dressed the frets, that sort of thing. Everything about that guitar is original. I have all of my bench notes from that visit, including pictures, so it'll be easy to identify the guitar if this is it."

"If you can easily identify it, why do you need me here?"

"I'm hoping you might recognize the guy who brings it in. From what I understand, it was stolen during a party that you hosted at Rudy's lodge."

"Something like that."

"Here's my plan," said Doug. "I'd like you to inconspicuously hang out in the showroom. Act like you're looking for a new guitar. Take a few for a test drive."

"We can do that."

"But keep your eyes peeled for anyone who comes upstairs carrying a guitar. None of the instruments up here are for sale, so the only person who would bring one up would be bringing it for an appraisal. And I have only that one appraisal scheduled."

"Okay. We'll give it our best shot."

They went back downstairs to the showroom. Tony enjoyed trying out some of the guitars. A Rickenbacker twelve-string especially caught his attention, so much so that Megan was concerned he wasn't watching the stairway. She staked out the adjacent area that held the acoustic guitars, where she could easily watch the main showroom without anyone even noticing she was there.

At four thirty Tony checked his watch. No one had come in carrying a guitar. He looked over at Megan. She shrugged her shoulders.

A few minutes later, a man in his early thirties, wearing a tan cap over a blond ponytail, walked into the store carrying something the size of a guitar wrapped in an old Green Bay Packers comforter. The person at the front counter directed him to the stairway that led to Doug's office.

As he disappeared onto the second floor, Megan hurried over to Tony.

"Do you think that's our guy?"

"I suppose it must be. He didn't act like he's been in here before, so I don't think he's a regular customer."

"I didn't recognize him," she said. "Have you seen him before?"

"No. Seems like someone we'd remember."

"Now what?"

"I guess we continue our stakeout until we get a signal from Doug."

About fifteen minutes later, Mr. Ponytail walked back down the stairs with a smile on his face and nothing in his arms. Without looking at anything else in the store, which was hard to do if you were a guitar player, he headed out the front door.

The phone rang at the front counter. A moment later the clerk came over to Tony and Megan and said that Doug would like to see them upstairs.

"Did you recognize him?" Doug asked, a vintage Stratocaster on a stand next to his desk.

"No," said Tony. "Neither of us recall ever seeing him before. Is that Rudy's guitar?"

"It is," Doug said, picking up the valuable instrument and handing it to Tony. "Lots of miles and love packed into this beauty."

"What happens now?" Megan asked.

"First off, let me say that there was no way I was letting that guy walk back out the door with this guitar. He had no idea what it was worth, so I offered him what he thought was a fair price—actually a fraction of its true value—but he seemed more than happy to take it. So I bought it from him."

Tony and Megan stood silently, unsure how to respond.

"I know what you're thinking," Doug said. "Don't worry, as far as I'm concerned, this is still Rudy's guitar, or at least it's now part of his estate. My goal was to get it back and off the street."

"What about the thief?" asked Megan.

"We'll work with the police regarding his selling stolen property. One of my guys went out and got pictures of his car and plates where he parked along the street. Looks like he was trying to avoid the cameras in our parking lot. We've also got him on surveillance cameras inside the store. Not the brightest guy in the world. I don't know what kind of operation he thinks I run here, but we certainly are not in the business of fencing stolen instruments."

"What happens to the guitar, now?" Tony asked. "Will it become part of your collection?"

"Honestly, I hope that someday it will. But right now, I'm handing it back to you. You mentioned when we talked earlier that you'd hoped to display it at Rudy's memorial tomorrow. That's a marvelous idea. I know he'd be honored."

"That's fantastic!" said Tony. "That's very generous of you." He began to carefully wrap the instrument in the comforter it had arrived in.

"Whoa, hold on. Don't think for a minute that I'm letting you leave with it wrapped in that old rag. Do you know if Rudy still had the case for it?"

"I do. I know right where it is, too. I'll make sure it's stored safely inside when we get back."

"Until then, we'll box it up for your trip home."

Doug reached out and shook Tony's and Megan's hands. "Thank you for coming over on such short notice."

"And thank you," said Tony. "You have no idea how much this means."

"Oh, I think I do," Doug said, scanning across his collection of vintage instruments. "Do me a favor and let the estate attorney know that I'm more than willing to pay a fair price so I can add it to my museum."

"Wow," said Megan as they pulled out of the parking lot, the boxed-up guitar hidden beneath the Packers comforter in the back. "I'm so glad that went well."

"Me too. And I'm relieved that we don't have to deal with the person who stole it. I'm curious who he was though."

"So am I. But that's not our worry."

Chapter 26

Even though it was late by the time they got back home from La Crosse, Megan could hardly wait to call Martha with the good news about retrieving Rudy's guitar.

"I told her we'll bring it along tomorrow afternoon," she told Tony. "Until then, I assured her that it'll never be out of our sight."

"Was she pleased to hear the good news?"

"I'd say so. She got so choked up it was hard to understand her response. As best as I could tell, she said 'thanks for letting us know.' Then she hung up."

"It'll be good to have the memorial over with," said Tony.

"Speaking of the memorial. I have one more idea. Very traditional and we'll have to work quickly."

"Okay, what are you volunteering me for this time?"

"You know those pictures that you took for the brochure. We could put together a photo board. If you're willing to pick up a tri-fold display board and some double-stick tape, I'd be willing to sort through the pictures and put it together. I should be able to get it done tomorrow morning, in time for the memorial."

"Sounds like a good idea. I shot a lot of pictures of him

that day. Most are posed, with the brochure in mind, but I also took a number of candids at various places around the resort. Only problem is, only a few of them are printed out."

"In that case, when you pick up the poster board and tape, get extra ink and photo paper, too."

"Okay. I'll put everything on a thumb drive so you can start going through them while I'm gone. I also have quite a few pictures that I shot during the murder mystery dinner that I haven't even looked at, yet. I'll put those on the drive, too."

"I realized we hadn't eaten any supper," Tony said when he returned with the photo board supplies, "so I picked up a couple of butter burgers. I hope you're hungry."

"Always. Thanks."

As they began eating, Megan scrolled through the images on the laptop in front of them.

"I noticed something interesting in a couple of the pictures."

"What's that?"

"I don't want to say until you look at them."

She clicked on one of the pictures taken during the murder mystery dinner.

"I thought you were looking for pictures of Rudy?" Tony asked.

"I was, but I also looked through the images from the dinner. Take a close look at this and tell me what you see."

She showed him the picture he'd taken of Elvis and Buddy talking together along the lakeshore.

"Oh, sure. They were discussing their favorite gauges of guitar strings. I wasn't sure if those two were actual guitarists or just getting into their characters. But, regardless, overhearing that conversation is what prompted me to add the guitar string to the crime scene."

"Take a look at the background of the picture. Back by the cabins."

She zoomed in. There were two people standing by the middle cabin, apparently talking to each other.

"I remember them. As soon as I headed toward the cabin, they disappeared."

"Look more closely."

She zoomed in on the pair.

"Now tell me what you see."

"Holy... That's the ponytail guy!"

"That's what I thought. And, it's hard to tell, but I'm guessing that the person he's talking to is Byrdie's guy, Thomas. They're right by their cabin."

"I'll bet they're planning how to steal Rudy's guitar."

"That'd be my guess. Here's another picture you need to look at."

She opened up an image taken earlier the same day, when the guests were first arriving. Several of the characters were chatting on the porch. The picture was artfully taken from inside the lodge, through the picture window, with the lake in the background.

"Hmmm, that turned out better than I expected," Tony commented. "I wasn't sure if the lighting would work."

"And what do you see specifically?"

"That the people are a bit dark, but the lake is exposed perfectly. Nothing that I couldn't fix in PhotoShop."

"Try again."

"That my composition is a little off? Byrdie is looking out at the water, not at the other guests."

"You're getting warmer. What is she looking at?"

"A pontoon boat going by."

Megan zoomed in on the boat.

"No way!" exclaimed Tony. "The driver is the ponytail guy!"

"Sure looks that way. The three of them must have been in cahoots to steal the guitar. While Byrdie had everyone's attention in the Great Hall, Thomas must have snuck the guitar out through the tunnel to the boathouse, where his long-haired, freaky-people friend was waiting with his boat."

"Nice folks," Tony said sarcastically. "Quite the way to thank Rudy for letting us use his resort for the mystery dinner. Not to mention, for giving those two a place to live."

"Do you suppose we should send a copy of these pictures to the police?"

"Let's hold off for now and see how things play out. If they ask us for more info, we can pass the pictures on then. In the meantime, let's keep our eyes open in case we see him again."

"And lets sleep with Rudy's guitar under our bed tonight."

Chapter 27

Megan got to work on the memory board first thing Saturday morning. The photos Tony had taken did a nice job of capturing Rudy's life in his Northwoods environment. It struck her as ironic that the pictures, which were intended for a brochure about leaving a legacy, were instead being displayed on his memory board.

"What do you think?" she asked Tony as he walked by.

"It's a nice tribute. Glad that you thought of it."

"I'm not sure this really qualifies as being a memory board," she said, "since all of these pictures were taken over just a few days. "

"It fits *our* memory of him."

"That's true. It's actually more of a day-in-the-life portrait of Rudy Rogers and the place he called home."

There was space for one more picture on the board.

"I need your opinion on this last picture," Megan said.

She held up a picture of Rudy on the stage in the boat house, tapping his cane on the floor.

"I love this picture," she said. "It almost looks like he's singing and dancing."

"He kinda was. He was singing an old Buddy Holly tune and tapping out the rhythm with his cane to show me how good the acoustics were. He was in his own little world. I hadn't seen him that happy anywhere else on the tour he gave me."

"It shows. But I'm wondering if I should include it. That's the spot, unfortunately, where we found him after his fall."

Tony thought for a moment.

"Include it. It makes me smile. Maybe this happy image will replace the unpleasant image stuck in my brain from when we found him."

"I wish I'd have been with you when he was showing you the dance hall. That sounds like a special moment."

"It was, especially for him. Obviously he was reliving a significant memory. The man looked like he was ready to plug in his guitar and blast off."

"Have you figured out how to plug the boom box into his amp?"

"I have, but we'll need to stop by the music store on the way through town to pick up an adapter cable. I called and they have one in stock. As long as the amp's in good working order, which I can't imagine it wouldn't be considering the way he kept up the guitar, it should work fine."

Megan stuck the last picture on the newly christened Day in the Life board.

I guess it's the quality of the memories that count, not the quantity, she thought.

A short time later, she put the picture board in the car next to the boom box and Rudy's Stratocaster, which was still wrapped in the Packers quilt.

The music store had the adapter waiting for Tony.

"Will you be stopping by the memorial this afternoon?" Tony asked the clerk.

"I'll be there. I have a feeling it could be a good turn out. A couple of older guys stopped in here this morning wanting to know where Foxglove Lodge was located. Said they knew him from his Rudy and the Rockets days and had just run into him weekend before last in Bayfield. Not sure how they found out about the memorial."

"I guess he wasn't as alone as it seemed."

"Hard to say. Aside from the day when he came in here with you trying to track down his guitar, he was always alone."

Tony paid for the adapter and rejoined Megan in the car.

"Did you get what you need?"

"I did. They had it sitting on the counter waiting for me. I hope it works okay. I hate waiting until the last minute."

"You can always just play it through the boom box. No one will be bothered by that except you."

"Maybe not only me. I just found out that a couple of guys who knew Rudy back in the day are going to be at the memorial."

Martha's car was already parked next to the lodge when they arrived. As expected, she seemed distracted.

"Would you help me set these cookies on a tray?" she said to Megan. "It seemed like we should have something for folks to nibble on. I heard that cranberry oatmeal were Rudy's favorites. I baked them this morning. I brought some bottles of raspberry tea, too."

"How many people are you expecting?"

"No idea. I just want to be prepared."

Tony told her that the guy at the music store said that a couple of Rudy's old friends were in town and planning to stop by.

Martha closed her eyes, took a deep breath and smiled just a little.

"I need to get a couple of things from Rudy's room," Tony said, stepping across the hall.

The first thing he grabbed was the empty guitar stand.

"Where would you like me to set Rudy's guitar?" he asked.

"I placed the urn and Rudy's mementos on the fireplace mantel," Martha replied. "How about on the hearth, front and center right beneath them?"

He set the stand in front of the fireplace, then went out to the car to get the guitar. Megan came along to retrieve the memory board. She also brought in the 45 RPM record of 'Tunnel of Love' that they'd found at the antique store.

Tony carefully positioned the instrument on the stand, immediately below the picture of Rudy and the Rockets that showed Rudy holding it. He couldn't help but chuckle as he looked at the autographs of the four musicians, recalling Rudy's story about how the girls in their fan club, not the band members themselves, had signed their publicity photos. Megan set the memory board and record next to the guitar, creating an interesting mix of then and now. Or at least as close to now as was possible.

"I need to take the boom box and amp down to the boat house," Tony said. "Will there be someone here to watch over the guitar while I'm gone?"

"We'll be here," said Megan. "Do you need any help with the amp?"

"I should be able to get it over there okay. It was designed to be lugged around."

Gripping the handle of the amp with one hand and the boom box with the other, he began his way down the path toward the boat house. Halfway there he was wishing that he'd packed the equipment into the car and driven. *These things must have gotten heavier over time*, he thought, setting the cabinet on the ground and shaking out the cramp in his hand.

Since he was already halfway to the boat house, it didn't make sense for him to lug the stuff back to the lodge and load it into the car. And he sure wasn't comfortable leaving it sitting unattended along the path.

After a short breather, he picked up the equipment and made it to the boathouse. As he got to the door, he hoped that the key was still hidden where he'd left it. It was. He unlocked the door and hesitated.

They had not been back here since the accident.

He brought the gear inside and set it on the stage. Then he scanned his surroundings. He was relieved to see that someone had cleaned up the blood at the front of the stage. The dance hall was bright and cheerful, sun streaming in the freshly cleaned windows. Perfect for a celebration of Rudy's life.

Tony set the amp on the front of the stage and connected the boom box. The adapter fit perfectly. Then he looked for somewhere to plug in the power cords. The only outlet was on the back wall and the power cords on the equipment were too short to reach.

He looked around to see if he could find an extension cord. No luck.

It's always the simplest things that go wrong, he thought. *Looks like I'm heading back to the lodge to see if I can find one there.*

He was halfway back to the lodge when it occurred to him that there might be an extension cord in Byrdie and Thomas' cabin. He went up and knocked on the door.

No answer.

He opened the unlocked door and called out: "Hello? Anyone home?"

The tiny cabin was empty. He didn't see any extension cords lying around just waiting for him to find them.

He stuck his head in the bedroom.

There were two single beds with a night stand between them. On the night stand was a lamp and a clock, both plugged into a power strip.

That's exactly what I need. But he wasn't comfortable taking it until he noticed something on one of the beds. Or, more precisely, something not on the bed.

The bed to the right of the night stand was covered with only a blanket. The other bed was covered with a comforter. A somewhat worn Green Bay Packers comforter that matched the one that had been wrapped around Rudy's guitar.

Those bastards!

He unplugged the lamp and clock and took the power strip, leaving the cabin door wide open when he left.

Chapter 28

Tony's first test of running the boom box through Rudy's old guitar amp didn't go as he'd hoped. The music came out at a decent volume, but there was a horrible buzzing coming through the speakers.

He disconnected it and played the music through the boom box without the amplifier. No hum, but also not nearly enough sound to fill the old dance hall.

He wiggled the cords to see if they might be loose. No change. He turned off the amplifier, disappointed.

Then he remembered that vintage guitar amplifiers often had an issue with their grounding. He unplugged the boom box and flipped the polarity switch on the back of the amp. He reconnected the boom box and switched it on.

"Yes!" he said out loud, raising his fist in the air. The sound was now loud and clear, worthy of an old rock 'n' roll band.

He played the tape through in its entirety to make sure there were no glitches, then rewound it to the beginning of 'Tunnel of Love.'

Well, he thought, *I don't suppose I can stall much longer. I'd better get back up to the lodge.*

He turned off the equipment and, just to be safe, also flipped off the power strip.

He was uncomfortable leaving the sound system unguarded in the boat house, but finally concluded that their suspected thieves would either have another key or know the alternate ways to get into the dance hall. He locked the door, but instead of returning the key to its hiding place, he put it in his pocket.

As he left the boathouse he noticed some orange marking ribbons tied to several of the trees, all in a row, that divided the resort property from the golf course. He didn't remember seeing them before. After spending longer than expected setting up the sound, though, he figured he'd better ignore them and get back to the lodge.

On the way back, he once again passed Byrdie and Thomas's cabin. The door was still open. He considered closing it, but was so mad about what they had done that he instead decided to make it even more obvious to them that they'd been found out. He went back inside, pulled the remaining Packers comforter off the second twin bed and dragged it out to the little porch at the front of the cottage. He spread it out over the railing where it couldn't be missed, then pulled out his phone and called Doug's guitar shop.

By the time he returned to the lodge, a number of cars were already parked alongside the old building. Beyond the lodge, at the far edge of the property, he noticed a couple more orange ribbons tied to the trees.

Just then, another car pulled in. Tony recognized the driver and waited for him. It was the Tuesday-morning librarian. They walked up the porch steps together.

"Glad to see you," said Tony. "Looks like a good turn-out."

"That's nice to see," said the librarian, looking around at the beautiful setting. "You know, for all of the times I've chatted with Rudy, I've never thought much about where he lived. To me, he existed at the check-out desk on Tuesday mornings. We've visited that way for the last couple of years. It's funny how different people have different memories of the same person."

"My memories of Rudy," said Tony, "are mostly right here at Foxglove Lodge and they only reach back a couple of weeks."

As they stepped inside the Great Hall, Tony recognized a number of the other mourners. Megan was near the door, welcoming guests and inviting them to sign a spiral-bound notebook that was on a small table near the entrance. A huge bouquet of foxglove flowers was prominently displayed on the table in a tall ceramic vase. A small sign was leaned against the bottom of the vase that read: 'Do Not Touch. Poisonous.' There was also a wooden box with a slot in the top in case someone wanted to leave their condolences. Absent from the table were any little memorial folders typically found at a funeral.

"I'd forgotten how much is involved in putting something like this together," Tony said to Megan. "Now I understand why Martha seemed so distracted. It was very thoughtful of her to step up and handle the details."

"Speaking of Martha, have you seen her?" asked Megan. "I haven't seen her since you left and I'm not sure how she's got things planned."

"She didn't come down to the boat house," Tony replied. Then he leaned close to his wife and whispered: "Come with me outside. I need to tell you something."

They went back out onto the front porch where they could talk without being overheard and he told her about finding the comforter in the cabin and that he had called the music store to tell them what he'd found.

"That kinda nails the lid on their coffin, doesn't it?" Megan said.

"Let's hope so. Are they here?"

"I haven't seen them."

"Since they weren't at their cabin, I thought they might have come to the memorial, them being Rudy's little angels and all."

"Would you be here if *you* were the prime suspects in a robbery?"

"I can't speak from experience," Tony quipped, "but I do know that in murder mysteries, the guilty party is always in the room with the other suspects when the sleuth exposes them as the killer."

"Not sure if that holds true for a robbery."

"Don't forget Rudy's book clues," said Tony. "This might be more than a robbery."

"If that's the case, are you going to play the all-knowing detective and solve his murder?"

"Maybe it'll unfold like the murder mystery dinner and one of the suspects will step forward and solve the case for us, like Byrdie solved the Weasel Leach murder."

"As I recall," Megan pointed out, "Byrdie solved it incorrectly. Didn't you tell me that in your script she was the person who actually killed Weasel Leach?"

"Good point." Tony thought for a moment, then exclaimed: "I've got it! I know what happened! The mystery dinner was a practice run for Byrdie, well, actually for Sarah. Maybe she attended the mystery dinner specifically to hone her skills at throwing someone else under the bus."

"Interesting theory. Let's both keep our eyes and ears open to see if any more clues materialize."

The room was soon filled with about two dozen guests. Several of the participants from the mystery dinner had shown up to pay their respects. It was odd seeing them without their '60s regalia. Tony and Megan decided to mingle with the guests and see what they could learn.

Chuck and Buddy showed up together. Tony discovered that they were co-workers at a business that renovated and built log homes. Their participation in the mystery dinner was primarily an excuse to get inside the historic lodge and study its construction. They also hoped to tell Rudy that if he decided to renovate the place, they were ready to offer their services. Now that he was gone, they admitted they'd be thrilled to take possession of the place if it came up for auction.

Tony also discovered that they both played guitar. Their discussion during the murder mystery dinner of the best guitar strings was legitimate.

Kenny from the history museum was there, as was the clerk from the music store. The woman who ran the homeless shelter, which Rudy had said he'd support in his will, was also part of the group.

Cher and Janis had arrived together. Megan learned that Cher was a lawyer in real life. In fact, she was the lawyer who would be reading Rudy's will.

Janis was a legal secretary at the same firm.

No wonder they seemed so comfortable together, thought Megan. *I hope they're better at lawyering than they were at playing the murder mystery game.*

There was no sign of Sonny. Megan remembered that he and Cher had arrived at the mystery dinner together.

There was no sign of Mama Bass, either, which surprised the couple since she was so outgoing and talkative at the murder mystery dinner.

"Maybe she doesn't like not being the center of attention," suggested Tony.

"Or, maybe, she's going to disprove your theory that the person who committed the crime is always at the denouement."

"Mama didn't strike me as the criminal type."

"Did Byrdie?"

"I haven't seen Elvis, either," said Tony. "I guess he really has left the building."

"You know, he's been sighted many times after his supposed death," Megan said, nodding knowingly. "I heard he's living in a nursing home under the name Bubba Hotep. He's probably one of the old rockers Rudy met up with at Bayfield."

Before Tony could add any more stupid comments to their banter, Martha appeared in the hall. She'd been in Rudy's room.

She stepped before the mourners.

"Thank you for coming," said Martha. "I know this is an unusual gathering. For many of us, Rudy Rogers was practically a stranger, but he left an impression on each of us in his own unique way."

As she was speaking, two old gentlemen stepped into the lodge. They stayed in the back, not far from Megan and Tony, leaning against the wall near the door.

They must be the guys who stopped at the music store, thought Tony.

Martha continued: "I only met Rudy about six weeks ago, when we were planning the library's expansion campaign. But I feel as if he's been part of my life much longer than that. Everyone who met Rudy Rogers took a liking to the man. I've heard that he even swept a few off their feet. One in particular, if you believe song lyrics."

The old guys at the back smiled, nodded and looked at each other knowingly.

"This will be an informal celebration of Rudy's life. Take a look at the pictures and mementos over by the fireplace."

"Just don't walk off with his guitar," quipped the man from the music store.

"Yes," said Martha. "Thanks to Tony and Megan, here, Rudy's Stratocaster has been safely returned, and we don't need to go through that again.

She put her hands together and led the group in applause.

"Also, be sure to grab a cookie and some tea. In about twenty minutes we'll all walk down to the boat house, where we'd love to hear your personal thoughts and stories about how Rudy affected your lives. Then the deceased's ashes will be cast into the wind.

"Following that, those of you who have an interest are asked to remain in the boathouse for the reading of the will. Thank you for being part of this celebration of Rudy

Roger's long and mysterious life."

As the others in the group mingled, the two old guys moved over to the fireplace to look at the mementos. They especially studied the band picture, pointing at the signatures and smiling.

"I'll bet those guys are Rudy's Rockets," Tony said to Megan. "They're probably laughing at their bogus autographs. I'd love to meet them. Maybe I could get them to autograph my record. With their real signatures."

"Well, fan boy, go over and introduce yourself."

Just then, Martha interrupted the couple and said to Tony: "Would you please take Rudy's guitar down to the boathouse. It'd be nice to have it down there as we give our final tribute. I'll bring the urn and the picture of Rudy and the Rockets."

"Sure thing," said Tony. "I need to go down there first, anyway, because I have the key." He reached into his pocket to make sure it was still there. "I'll get the case for the guitar."

He walked down the hall to Rudy's room, took a deep breath and gently opened the door. As he slowly stepped inside, he scanned the old man's lifetime of musical memories. Even without the personal items that were displayed on the fireplace, it was still an impressive collection.

He pushed aside the tie-dyed curtain that hid the closet filled with cases and other musical gear. The original tweed case for the Stratocaster was in the front, right where he'd remembered Rudy putting it when he first visited the old rocker. He took the case from the closet, pulled the curtain shut and went back into the Great Hall.

Megan and Martha both joined him at the fireplace. He lay the case on the hearth and opened the lid. There were still various papers and envelopes at the bottom of the case. Tony removed the guitar from its stand and carefully placed it into the case.

The open case with the guitar inside, its plush-covered lid raised up like the lid of a coffin, changed the ambience in the room from a celebration of Rudy's life to a solemn viewing of a body at a wake.

"Megan," he asked, shaking the image from his head, "would you come with me to the boat house and carry the stand?"

Megan picked up the guitar stand as Tony reverently closed the lid on the case.

"We'll meet you down at the dance hall in a few minutes," Martha said as Tony and Megan left the lodge, quite possibly for the last time.

Chapter 29

"Looks like they've returned to the scene of the crime," said Tony as they walked past Byrdie and Thomas's cabin.

The Packers comforter was no longer hanging over the porch railing and the cabin door was closed.

"Can't say that I'm glad to see that," said Megan. "I'm not crazy about having to confront them."

"I don't see a vehicle here. Maybe they've come and gone."

"We can hope."

When they got to the boat house, Tony listened at the door. All was quiet.

He set the guitar case down and took the key out of his pocket.

"You ready?"

Megan nodded.

He undid the lock, then put the key back in its hiding spot.

He picked up the case with his left hand, turned the latch with his right and slowly pushed open the door.

They looked at each other, then stepped inside.

Everything was as Tony had left it forty-five minutes

earlier. Megan set the stand in front of the amplifier, next to the boom box.

Tony laid the case on the floor in front of the curtain near the back of the stage and opened the lid. He took out the instrument and carefully set it on the stand.

"There you go, Mr. Stratocaster," he said. "You're back where it all began."

Tony and Megan sat down at the edge of the stage, their feet barely touching the floor. They were only a few feet away from where they'd found Rudy. For a minute or two, neither said a word.

Then Megan suddenly asked: "Where was Rudy's cane when we found him?"

"On the stage, right behind where we're sitting. Why?"

"In every one of the pictures that you took of Rudy, he's holding his cane. He always had it in his right hand."

"So it makes sense that he'd have it with him when he fell."

"Yes, but why did it end up behind him? If he accidentally slipped off the edge of the stage, the cane would have slipped off first and ended up on the dance floor. You always place the cane ahead of yourself when you're walking. And it was his right arm that was hanging over the edge of the stage. But Rudy's cane was behind him. That doesn't make any sense."

Tony looked behind himself to the spot where the cane was found, a few feet behind where they sat. "Do you suppose someone found him before we did and moved the cane?"

"Or... they snuck up behind him and somehow pulled the cane backwards out from under him, causing him to fall forward, hitting the edge of the stage. Then the person left the cane where it fell and fled."

"Either way, they left Rudy here to die."

"So we *are* looking at a murder. But why was Rudy down here in the first place? And who would want him dead?"

"I think we were correct when we suspected that he'd heard someone in the lodge, saw that they'd left through the tunnel and followed them down here."

"And when he got here," Tony finished, "they were waiting for him behind the curtain."

Tony got up and walked to the back of the stage. He quickly pulled aside the back curtain. No one was behind it.

"Look at that," said Megan, pointing to a long pole with a hook on it that was resting against the back wall. "What's that for?"

"I think it's for opening and closing the sky lights."

"It'd work really well for reaching out from behind the curtain and hooking the cane of an old man who was standing near the edge of the stage. I think we found our murder weapon."

Just then, Martha and the rest of the mourners began filing into the dance hall. Tony and Megan returned the pole, closed the curtain and hopped off the stage to meet them.

Martha silently acknowledged the couple, then stepped up onto the stage and set the signed picture of Rudy and the Rockets in front of the guitar. *Something looks different about that picture,* thought Tony.

Next, Martha reverently placed the urn on the stage.

She crossed herself and draped a string of rosary beads over the wooden urn.

"I guess Rudy must have been Catholic," Tony whispered to Megan, once again recognizing how little he knew about the man.

"Looks that way," she said. "I wonder why he didn't have a church funeral."

Martha checked something at the back of the stage, behind the curtain, as the others filled the dance hall.

Megan noticed that most of the people who'd been up at the lodge had come down to the boat house.

"Looks like everyone but the two old guys are here," Megan quietly commented to Tony.

"They probably didn't want to walk this far," he replied. "It was nice that they came at all. I'm disappointed I didn't get a chance to talk with them."

Martha stepped up to the front of the stage.

"We made it!" she said. "It's amazing how much farther things seem when you get old. Let me thank you again for being part of this celebration of Rudy's life.

"I first met Rudy when I approached him about using his place for our murder mystery dinner. He seemed surprised that any of us even knew that he lived at Foxglove Lodge or knew anything about him beyond his regular use of the library."

As she continued speaking, two more people quietly stepped into the dance hall. Instead of joining the others near the front of the stage, they lingered near the door.

It was Sarah and Thomas.

They did not look happy.

Chapter 30

"My mother was a big fan of early rock 'n' roll," Martha continued, standing on the stage in the dance hall. "Mom loved to reminisce about the bands that she'd seen as a teenager, many right here in the Northwoods. She was always telling me stories about a place called Crystal Rock Ballroom. By the time I was old enough to go there, The Rock, as we called it, was a roller rink, but back in the day, my mom and her friend Karen saw Johnny Cash, Carl Perkins, and the Everly Brothers under The Rock's crystal chandelier. The act she talked about most, though, was Buddy Holly and the Crickets.

"She saw Buddy in 1958, the year before he died in that horrible plane crash. Besides his songs, he's now known for being one of the first musicians to play a Fender Stratocaster guitar, just like this one.

She pointed to Rudy's guitar behind her.

"Rudy patterned his band, Rudy and the Rockets, after Buddy Holly and the Crickets.

"Rudy and the Rockets played here on August 4, 1962, in this dance hall, on this very stage. I know that because Mom kept a scrapbook of her musical memories. She'd saved pictures of her favorite artists, which included some photos that she'd taken herself. There were also newspaper ads for the various shows she'd attended. Among the clippings was an ad for Rudy and the Rockets at Foxglove Lodge. That's how I know the date they were here.

"When my mother passed away last year, she left behind a box of treasured mementos, neatly tied up with a satin ribbon. One of the treasures inside that box was a signed publicity photo of Rudy and the Rockets. I was surprised that it wasn't in the scrapbook with her other memories."

Martha stepped back and picked up the picture that was sitting in front of Rudy's guitar.

"This is not the same picture that you looked at up in the lodge. That picture, which I found among Rudy's treasured items, was signed by all four of the members of his band.

"This picture, the picture that my mom had hidden away in her private memories box, was signed by only one of the band's members."

She read aloud:

> *To Annie—*
> *Love, Rudy Rogers.*

"My mother, Annie, was working here at Foxglove Lodge the summer of '62. It was her first job out of high school. She was only eighteen years old."

Several folks in the room shifted uncomfortably.

She set the picture back in front of the guitar.

"Mom never mentioned the name Rudy Rogers. It wasn't until she passed away and I found this picture that the name caught my attention. I decided to learn more about this mysterious fellow and his band. Thank heavens for YouTube and rock fans with too much time on their hands."

A few people chuckled.

"I found a podcast that did deep dives into the history of old, regional rock bands. One of the bands featured was Rudy and the Rockets. They were only together for a few years, but they had a couple of songs that made it into the Top Forty. One was called 'Outta Space' and the other 'Blast Off.' You might have heard them in the sound tracks of TV commercials and under movie credits, without giving any thought to who recorded them.

"The podcast host loved trivia about the songs and artists that he featured and told an interesting story about the flip side of 'Blast Off.' The song was called 'Tunnel of Love.' According to the story, band leader Rudy Rogers wrote the song about a girl that he met at a resort in Wisconsin. The resort had a dance hall above a boat house and there was a secret tunnel that connected that boat house to the main lodge. Sound familiar?"

Tony nodded knowingly and smiled at Megan.

"After their show," Martha continued, "the girl, who worked at the resort, snuck Rudy up to her room through the tunnel. The next day he wrote the song 'Tunnel of Love' and declared to his band mates that he'd found his soul mate, his one true love. According to the podcast, no one knows who the young lady was or what ever became of her."

Martha looked at the audience and shrugged.

"My mother never told me who my father was. She raised me on her own. All I know is that her 'good Catholic mother,' my grandmother, didn't want anything to do with a wayward daughter or a bastard grandchild and sent her to a home in another state to have her baby.

"When my mom returned with me, just an infant, she found that she was no longer welcome at her home. Even her church, which had been important to her, preferred that she remain invisible.

"My grandfather, God bless his soul, found a little house in the woods where Mom could raise me.

"My mother was a marvelous person. I loved her dearly. My only complaint, as I mentioned, was that she never told me who my father was. I had no clue until she died and I opened her memory box.

"Now, I know that an autographed picture isn't proof that Rudy Rogers was my father, but I was born in early May 1963. Do the math."

The folks in the room shifted uncomfortably. This was not the celebration of Rudy's life they were expecting.

"Last spring," Martha continued, "I discovered that a man named Rudy Rogers was living up here at Foxglove Lodge. Was it the same Rudy Rogers?

"I learned that the man was a regular patron of the library. I asked the librarian if he knew Rudy Rogers and he said that Rudy stopped in every Tuesday to pick up books that he'd put on hold. He didn't know much else about the elderly gentleman, but confirmed that he was, in fact, the same fellow who'd been in a rock band back in the '60s.

"The following Tuesday, I spent the morning doing research on the library computer. All the while, I was watching to see if Rudy came in to get his books.

"Sure enough, he showed up like clockwork. He was

older than I'd imagined him. Instead of a guitar slinging rocker, I was looking at an elderly man with a lovely
smile who walked with a cane."

She paused, then added emphatically. "He did not look
like the sort of person who would have gotten a young
girl pregnant and then abandoned her. And her baby. His
baby!"

She stepped to the side of the stage and grabbed a bottle of water.

As she slowly removed the cap and took a drink, calming herself, several of the folks in the room pulled out
chairs and sat down. It was obvious, her story wasn't
over. Sarah and Thomas stepped further into the room to
better hear what she was saying.

"I needed to know more about Rudy Rogers," Martha
continued. "As a member of the Friends of the Library's
fundraising committee, I suggested that we invite Rudy
to help us with our endowment campaign. Much to my
surprise, he agreed. He told the committee that as a regular patron of the library, he was already planning to leave
money to the library in his will, so being part of the committee would be a perfect fit.

"The Friend's committee liked my idea of hosting a
murder mystery dinner and—what a surprise!—we
needed someplace to hold it. I suggested that we try to
find someplace old, with an air of mystery. Someplace
with a Northwoodsy feel. Someplace like an old resort."

She smiled.

"Rudy took the bait. He offered to let us use Foxglove
Lodge, but preferred not to be involved in the actual pro-
duction of the event. I decided that I could work with

that. Of course, I'd need help."

She nodded in Megan and Tony's direction.

"Megan, here, conveniently volunteered Tony to write the script for our murder mystery dinner. To do that, he'd need to study the lodge so he'd know where to hide the clues. And then, to add frosting to the cake, he also agreed to take pictures of Rudy here at the resort for our brochure.

"Thank you, Tony! You did a great job of scoping out the entire place. I was especially interested to learn from you that there really was, and still is, a secret tunnel from the lodge to the boat house.

"And thank you Megan for helping me with the food preparation. The two of you made it so easy for me to inconspicuously get inside the lodge and learn more about Rudy without him suspecting a thing. We made a great team."

"Is she about to confess to Rudy's murder?" Megan whispered to Tony.

"If she is, I'm not thrilled that she's making us sound like her accomplices."

"Did you know that for ninety-nine dollars you can get a paternity test?" Martha asked rhetorically, her eyes quickly scanning the room.

"All you need are two tooth brushes, one from the child and one used by the alleged father. Mail them in and three days later you get back the results by email. Simple as that."

So that's what happened to Rudy's toothbrush, thought Tony.

"But damn it! Three days was too late! I got the email

confirming that Rudy was my father just a few hours after Megan and Tony found him slumped over this stage."

She took another drink.

I wonder what she has in that bottle, thought Tony.

"Sorry for going on and on," she said calmly. "Does anyone else have any *fun* stories to tell? This is supposed to be a celebration!"

Everyone remained silent.

Martha set down the bottle on the floor behind her, wrapped the rosary around her hand and picked up the urn.

"No one? Then I guess it's about time to scatter these ashes."

Chapter 31

Martha stepped off the stage with the urn cradled in her arms and purposefully walked through the crowd to the far end of the dance floor, where a glass door led to the large deck overlooking the lake.

"Please join me," she said, holding open the door.

Everyone in the room obediently and silently followed her instructions. The deck was crowded, but it seemed solid enough.

Martha quietly stepped through the hushed crowd to the edge of the deck and lovingly rested the urn on the railing.

"Dear God," she said, looking up to the beautiful, cloud-filled sky, "it is never easy to accept the loss of a loved one. But even in pain, we know that all things work together for good."

She removed the lid from the urn.

Oh crap! thought Tony. *This is when I'm supposed to switch on the music.*

He turned to make his way through the crowd. Martha, noticing the movement, glanced at him and smiled, then continued: "Dust to dust; ashes to ashes; we release your soul into God's loving hands."

As Martha cast the ashes into the wind, the opening chords of 'Tunnel of Love' suddenly filled the air.

Tony, still on the deck, turned his head along with everyone else and stared inside the dance hall. Standing next to the boom box, grinning from ear to ear, stood the two old guys.

By the time the song ended, everyone was back in the dance hall.

"Sorry it took us so long to get down here," said the taller of the two. "Old fellows like us don't move as fast as we used to. Did we miss anything?"

Chapter 32

Tony immediately went over to talk to the two gentleman.

"Thank you for covering my butt," he said. "I'm the one who was supposed to start the music, but I got so caught up in Martha's speech that I forgot until it was too late."

"Glad that we could help."

They acknowledged that they were in fact the surviving members of Rudy's Rockets: Matt McGregor, rhythm guitar, and Brian Aldean, bass. Their drummer, Billy Tucker had passed away a dozen years ago. They told Tony that Martha had mentioned to them up at the lodge that she was planning to play 'Tunnel of Love' when she dispersed the ashes.

"When we finally got to the boat house, everyone was already on the deck," said Matt. "We noticed the cassette player on the stage and saw Martha holding the urn up over the railing, but we didn't see anyone there to turn on the music, so without thinking, I hit the play button."

"Thanks again," said Tony, shaking their hands. "I'm so excited to meet you, I just found a copy of your single 'Blast Off' and 'Tunnel of Love' at an antique store."

"Well that says it all, doesn't it?" said Brian.

"After we're done here," asked Tony, "would you guys be willing to autograph it for me?"

"We'd be honored," said Matt.

"Would you prefer our real signatures," Brian joked, "or should we try to match the signatures created by our fan club? We got a kick out of seeing that old publicity photo up at the lodge. Brought back lots of great memories."

"When I saw the two of you studying that picture, I had a hunch it was you," said Tony. "How'd you hear about the memorial today?"

"Well, we, quite by chance, ran into Rudy last weekend at the oldies concert in Bayfield," said Matt. "The two of us both live in Duluth, so we see each other fairly often, but neither of us had seen Rudy in years."

"Not since before he bought this lodge," added Brian. "We had a great time reminiscing."

"Rudy decided to stay an extra night so we could spend the next day together," said Matt. "Before he left, we exchanged contact info and he made us promise to come down here sometime to see him.

"Then two days ago, I got a call from someone named Martha—I had no idea who she was until today—who asked that we come here for his celebration of life. We'd been laughing and joking with him just a few days earlier, so it was quite a shock."

"I've got to ask," said Tony. "Is the story about 'Tunnel of Love' true? When you played up here a zillion years ago, did Rudy really have a fling with the resort's housekeeper?"

They both laughed.

"The poor boy was smitten," said Matt. "He noticed her in the audience while we were barely into our first set. During each of our breaks, they chattered on like long-lost friends and at the end of our show, they simply vanished. We didn't know about any secret tunnel and had no idea where Rudy disappeared to."

"We were a little miffed that he didn't stick around to help tear down the equipment," added Brian. "That wasn't like him. The resort owners had provided lodging for the band that night in one of their little cabins—I think there were more of them back then—but we didn't see Rudy again until the next day."

"We didn't get back on the road until late afternoon," said Matt. "Turns out the love birds had snuck off in a rowboat and had a picnic on a little island at the other end of the lake. If we'd have known that we'd be here most of the day, we'd have played a round or two of golf."

"The poor boy was head over heals for her," added Brian. "He wrote the lyrics to 'Tunnel of Love' as we were driving to our next gig."

"Did he stay in touch with her?" asked Tony.

"I don't think he even knew her last name. I remember that he sent her some postcards, simply addressed to Annie c/o Foxglove Resort, but I have no idea if she ever received them. Since we were on the road for the next six months, there was no way for her to contact him. I don't have a clue what happened to her."

"You really should have gotten down here sooner," said Tony. "You missed the big reveal."

Just then, the lawyer, who Tony and Megan thought

of as Cher, stepped to the center of the room. She had in her hand the file folder marked Last Will and Testament, written in Sharpie. It was the folder that Tony and Megan had seen Sarah and Thomas looking at in Rudy's room shortly after they'd found the man slumped over the stage.

"Everyone who has an interest please stay for the reading of Rudy's will," said the lawyer. "Pull up a chair and make yourself comfortable."

"We don't need to be part of this," Matt said to Tony. "We'll catch you after you're done here. I'm hoping to take Rudy's old Strat for a spin before we leave."

"That should be no problem," said Tony. "The amp's already here and I noticed that there's a cable in the case."

Everyone else decided to stay in the dance hall.

The lawyer's assistant, known to Tony and Megan as Janis, positioned a chair in the middle of the room for the lawyer. She looked at her boss for approval that she'd put it in the right spot. The others pulled their chairs into a two-deep semi-circle facing the lawyer.

Megan pulled up a chair next to her for Tony, who had walked out with the band members.

"I saved you a seat, fan boy," she grinned when he returned.

Tony looked around the circle. "This reminds me of Sunday school when I was a kid. How about you?"

"The only time I went to Sunday school was one Easter when we visited my cousin in Iowa and I had to tag along. Considering it was called 'school,' there wasn't anything new to learn. We'd all heard the Easter story before."

"But, you've got to admit, that's one of the better Bible

stories. There's suspense, betrayal, back-room deals and a surprise ending worthy of Agatha Christie."

Once everyone was situated, the lawyer sat down with the folder on her lap.

She cleared her throat to get everyone's attention.

"Thank you for being here," she said,

It was hard to not think of her as Cher, the murder mystery character who simply ignored the rules and did whatever she pleased.

"I looked at the will briefly," she began, "and I don't think this should take long. Everything seems straight forward and in order."

She opened the folder and began reading from the document inside:

I, Rudolf James Rogers, being of sound mind, not acting under duress or undue influence, and fully understanding the nature and extent of all my property and of this disposition thereof, do hereby make, publish, and declare this document to be my Last Will and Testament, and hereby revoke any and all other wills and codicils heretofore made by me.

I nominate and appoint Sandra Marie Bournier, attorney at law, as personal representative of my estate.

"I'm Sandra, by the way. I guess I should have introduced myself earlier."

She nodded to Janis.

"This is my assistant, Cassidy Johnson. Now, on to the section of the will that I suspect you are most interested in, the disposition of property.

I devise and bequeath my property, both real and personal and wherever situated, as follows:

1st Beneficiary: For their marvelous service to the community as a whole and for their friendship to me personally, I bequeath to the Northwoods Public Library the amount of $10,000.

Tony looked over at the librarian. He smiled, but seemed a bit disappointed.

2nd Beneficiary: For the continuing good that they do by serving the homeless residents of our community, I bequeath to the Open Arms Homeless Shelter the amount of $10,000.

The director of the home seemed pleased.

3rd Beneficiary: For the wonderful and unwavering friendship they've shown me and for their loving dedication to caring for my ever-increasing needs, to my little angels, Sarah Sinclair and Thomas Williamson, I bequeath the amount of $100,000 to be split evenly between them.

Sarah and Thomas relaxed in their chairs, glanced at each other and grinned. The others in the room looked at them in silence, perplexed. The lawyer quickly moved on.

4th Beneficiary: So that Foxglove Resort may be restored to it's original glory and footprint, I bequeath the resort, it's buildings, contents and land to...

Kenny, director of the historical museum, sat up in his chair. He looked both excited and apprehensive.

...I bequeath the resort, it's buildings, contents and land to the Apex Land Development Company.

There was an audible gasp from those in the room, then complete silence. The lawyer, doing her best to contain a smile, continued reading.

If any of my beneficiaries have pre-deceased me, then any property that they would have received if they had not pre-deceased me shall be distributed in equal shares to the remaining beneficiaries.

Except to the extent that I have included them in this Will, I have intentionally, and not as a result of any mistake or inadvertence, omitted in this Will to provide for any family members and/or issue of mine, if any, however defined by law, presently living or hereafter born or adopted.

Megan looked at Martha, who stared straight ahead, her face revealing no emotion.

My Personal Representative, shall have and may exercise all discretionary powers in addition to any common law or statutory powers without the necessity of court license or approval.

I, the undersigned Rudolf James Rogers, do hereby declare that I sign and execute this instrument as my last Will, that I sign it willingly in the presence of each of the undersigned witnesses, and that I execute it as my free and voluntary act for the purposes herein expressed.

"The document has been duly signed and dated by the

decedent and witnessed by Willis Chadbourne and Cynthia Shroeder."

The lawyer closed the document and placed it back inside the folder.

"Does anyone have any questions?

Tony shifted uncomfortably in his seat, looked to Megan for support, then raised his hand.

Chapter 33

All eyes shifted in Tony's direction.

"Could you repeat who witnessed the will?"

The lawyer opened the folder and scanned down to the end of the document.

"The witnesses were Willis Chadbourne and Cynthia Schroeder of Mapleford, Wisconsin. It was witnessed and dated when it was signed by Rudolf Rogers."

With a quick glance toward Sarah and Thomas, she put the will back in the folder.

"The reason I'm asking," said Tony, "is that just a couple weeks ago, Rudy and I were talking about writing a will, and he told me that pretty much anyone could witness the signing of the document, as long as they weren't included as beneficiaries."

"That is correct. And that is clearly what he's done." She looked away from Tony and addressed the group as a whole. "Thank you, everyone, for coming here this after..."

"Just one more thing," Tony interrupted, feeling a bit like the old TV detective Columbo. "Rudy told me that he had his will witnessed by Sarah and Thomas."

"Obviously, he realized, after talking with you, that

since Sarah and Thomas were beneficiaries, they couldn't serve as his witnesses, so he redrafted the document and had it witnessed by someone else. It's a good thing that he had that discussion with you or the will would be invalid."

The rest of the folks in the room seemed intrigued by this discussion and remained in their seats.

"What would happen to the resort if the will was declared invalid?" Megan asked.

"Then it would go to the probate court and most likely the resort and other assets would be put up for auction at a sheriff's sale."

"Could I see the will?" Tony asked.

"I'm sorry, but no."

"I'd like to look at it, too," jumped in Kenny. "I was told by Rudy that the museum would be included in the will."

"Neither of you have the right to see the will," said the lawyer, "since neither of you are beneficiaries. I believe we're done here."

The librarian spoke up.

"I'm here representing the library, which is included as a beneficiary, and I would like to take a look at the document."

"You can set up an appointment with Cassidy and we can look at it together in my office."

She handed the folder to Cassidy.

"Why put it off when we're all here now?" said the librarian. "Do the other affected parties have any objections to my looking at the will?"

"I'm fine with that," said Kenny.

"It's okay with me, too," said the woman from the homeless shelter.

Everyone looked at Sarah and Thomas.

"Why the hell not?" said Sarah, smiling. "Seems like we're doing okay."

"That still leaves Apex Land Development," said the lawyer. "Unfortunately, their president was unable to join us today. Since they have no representative here, your request to see the document is denied."

The librarian had been doing some quick research on his phone. He was skilled at searching the records of businesses and corporations and easily found what he was looking for.

"That's not quite true," he spoke up. "I found Apex Land Development's records of incorporation, which was just last year, by the way. I also found their website, which is most informative. It even includes pictures of their president and board of directors."

"Could I see that?" asked Megan.

The librarian passed the phone to her.

"This *is* interesting," Megan said, studying one of the pictures and showing it to Tony. He nodded his head.

"You are correct," Megan said to the lawyer. "The president of Apex Land Development is not here today. But he *was* here the night of the murder mystery dinner. He was dressed as Sonny and arrived with the woman dressed as Cher... you!"

"So what?" snapped the lawyer. "We both happened to be at the same event to support the library. Big deal. There's nothing wrong with donating to a good cause."

Megan scrolled down Apex's page.

"According to this," she said, "you are legal counsel for Apex and a member of their land acquisition team. Kinda seems like a conflict of interest, doesn't it?"

"It just means that Rudy Rogers held me in such high regard that he not only trusted the future of his resort to Apex, but also had confidence in my being able to serve as executor of his estate. There's nothing criminal about that. We're done here." She stood up. "I've got nothing to hide."

"In that case," said the librarian, "I'd like to see the will."

Before the lawyer could object again, he stepped over to Cassidy, who looked up at the lawyer, then reluctantly handed him the folder. He glanced at it, then brought it over to Tony and Megan.

The three of them quickly studied the document.

"I'll be back in a second," said Tony, jumping up and hurrying to the side of the stage where he'd left the guitar case.

The librarian googled Mapleford and the names of the witnesses, then showed Megan an article from the local newspaper that included their pictures.

"Looks like the witnesses actually do exist," he announced. "I just found an article reporting that Willis Chadbourne and Cynthia Shroeder of Mapleford recently won their division in the state bowling tournament. It even includes their pictures proudly holding their trophies."

Cassidy squirmed uncomfortably in her seat.

"Thank you for confirming that," said the lawyer. "So, no problem then."

"No problem," said Megan, "except that Willis Chadbourne and Cynthia Shroeder of Mapleford, Wisconsin, won their trophies in the middle-school division. They're sixth graders!"

The lawyer glared at Cassidy and mumbled. "You couldn't even come up with the names of two adults!? You're fired!"

Chapter 34

Tony opened the guitar case. He was relieved to see that the documents were still inside. He lifted up the envelope that had 'will' written on the front. Under the envelope, he noticed a sheet of yellowing paper, torn from a spiral-bound notebook, with handwriting on it. He grabbed that, too.

On his way back across the stage, he picked up the picture of Rudy and the Rockets. Actually there were two pictures, one behind the other. Martha had brought them both to the boat house, the one signed to Annie and the other with all four signatures.

"What'd you get?" asked Megan.

"Rudy's *actual* will," he said loud enough so everyone could hear, holding up the document. "When he was showing me around a couple of weeks ago, he mentioned that he kept his most important papers in his guitar case. Said he figured that if he needed to leave in an emergency and only had time to grab one thing, he'd likely grab the guitar."

Several of those in the dance hall, including Kenny and the woman from the homeless shelter, gathered around Tony as he opened the new document.

Tony immediately flipped forward to the end of the will, where it was signed and witnessed.

"This will was witnessed by Sarah and Thomas," Tony said, "just like Rudy told me."

"That's 'cause he knew we were honest and he trusted us," said Thomas. "Rudy was an okay guy."

Byrdie glared at him, wishing he'd keep his mouth shut.

Tony looked through the document more closely and reported on what he found.

"The estate is divided up between the library, the homeless shelter and the historical museum," he said. "There's no mention in here of Sarah and Thomas inheriting anything, so their witnessing the document is appropriate. There's no mention of Apex Land Development, either."

The lawyer leaned close to her assistant and whispered in her ear: "Why didn't you get rid of that one?"

"I couldn't find it," she answered in her tiny little voice that reminded Tony of Betty Boop."

"Did you even look?"

"What difference does it make? The new will overrides the old one anyway."

The lawyer leaned away from Cassidy and spoke up for all to hear.

"What this gentleman has found is obviously an earlier draft of Mr. Roger's will, which has no bearing on our discussion here today."

Tony couldn't help but suddenly picture Rudy sitting on a chair putting on his sneakers.

"I'm sure that if you look at it," she continued, "you'll see that this document is dated prior to the will that I've presented."

Tony compared the dates.

"You are correct" he said. "This will that I found in the guitar case is dated about two months before the other one, which was dated only ten days ago."

"So, obviously," the lawyer stated, "he changed his mind. His health was deteriorating and he recognized that the generous and loving care he was receiving from this young couple should be rewarded."

She looked at Sarah and Thomas, who moved out of their seats and were now leaning against the windows at the side of the ballroom closest to the door.

"Thank you for watching over him during these last few months. He obviously appreciated what you did for him. He loved you."

Sarah looked like she was about to cry. Thomas smiled and gave a thumbs-up sign.

"There's something else about these two documents that intrigues me," said Tony, holding the last pages of each side by side and comparing them. He indicated to Megan what he'd found and she nodded her understanding.

"What conspiracy theory are you concocting now?" the lawyer said, staring daggers at those huddling over the wills.

"Rudy apparently changed more than his mind between signing the first and second wills," Megan said. "Either that or someone needs to work on their penmanship. The two signatures don't match."

The lawyer looked to Cassidy for an explanation.

"That's definitely Rudy's signature," the assistant said confidently, standing up and stepping over to Tony. "If you don't believe me, you can compare it to his signature on the autographed picture of his band."

She grabbed the pictures that Tony had brought back from the stage. She held up the one signed by the whole band.

"See," she said proudly. "They're the same. A perfect match."

"How about we compare the signatures on the will with the other photo?" said Tony.

He held the two side by side.

Cassidy looked at the pictures and the signatures on the two wills.

"Obviously," she said, "his signature changed over time."

"Changed pretty quickly," said Megan. "The wills are dated only a few months apart."

"Probably due to his deteriorating condition," chimed in the lawyer.

"I have it on good authority that the four signatures on the band photo were signed by members of their fan club, not by the band members themselves. So unless one of those fan members showed up to sign this will, someone else used that photo and tried to duplicate Rudy Roger's signature. I'm kinda thinking it was the latter."

"That's ridiculous," said the lawyer, "and unless you can get those fan girls here to verify what you're asserting, this is hearsay and legally worthless."

"We can clear this up quickly," said Tony. "Two of Rudy's band mates are here today. They can verify who autographed the picture. They're waiting outside. I'll go get them."

Tony handed the papers to Megan, stood up and scurried out the door.

A minute later he returned. Alone.

"They aren't out there," he reported. "I guess they got tired of waiting and left."

"Nice try," said the lawyer.

"That still leaves the signature on the first will," said Megan, who'd been thumbing through the papers that Tony had handed her when he rushed outside.

"There's a page of lyrics here, for the song 'Tunnel of Love.' It is handwritten and dated and signed by Rudy Rogers."

For the first time during this discussion, Martha seemed interested. She got up and hurried over to Megan.

"Could I see that?" she asked gently.

She studied the page, her lips silently forming the words as she read. She began to cry. Her hands shaking, she returned the page to Megan.

The signature on the lyric sheet and the signature on the picture that was autographed 'To Annie— Love Rudy Rogers' were perfect matches.

They even appeared to have been written with the very same pen.

Chapter 35

"Where are you going?" Megan called when she noticed Sarah and Thomas heading for the door, the lawyer and Cassidy close behind.

As Sarah reached for the door handle, the door suddenly opened on its own.

It was the county deputy.

"Hold on there," he said, blocking them from leaving. "We have information that a valuable guitar was recently stolen at this resort and that we should come and check it out. No one's leaving until I have a chance to find out what's going on."

Sarah glared at Thomas.

"What the hell were you thinking!?" she grumbled under her breath to him. "And why would you get that idiot friend of yours involved? Six months of work and you throw it all away for a stupid guitar! You should have stayed on script! Robbery was never part of the plan."

"Neither was murder!"

"I didn't murder anybody."

"Right, like I believe you. You probably called the cops on me for stealing the guitar to deflect suspicion away from you for offing the old guy."

"I had no reason to do that. Besides, you were with me when he was discovered on the stage."

"So? He'd already been laying there for awhile. You could have done it before you brought me back as your alibi. It's not like I monitor your actions minute by minute."

"Obviously I should have monitored yours during the murder mystery dinner."

The others had crowded toward the entryway to see what was going on.

"All of you, back inside," said the deputy. "Please sit down while I get to the bottom of this."

Once everyone was settled, he pulled out a notebook and asked: "Could someone describe the instrument that was stolen."

"No need to describe it," said Tony pointing to the stage, "it's sitting right... ."

There was no guitar on the stage.

"It was there a minute ago, I swear," said Tony. "It was right there with the amplifier and boom box. It was sitting on that stand."

He looked at the others in the room. "You saw it, right?"

Everyone nodded in agreement.

"It's been sitting there on the stage since we arrived," asserted the clerk from the music store.

"Well, that's not completely true," said Tony to the officer. "First it was up at the lodge, and then I carried it down here for Rudy's celebration of life. It was his guitar. And now it is gone. Again."

"Let me get this straight," said the deputy. "the old guitar was ..."

"It wasn't any old guitar," corrected Tony. "It was a vintage, valuable, irreplaceable instrument with a musical pedigree. That's why it ended up at Doug's Guitar shop. I'm assuming they're the ones who contacted you."

"So the vintage, valuable, irreplaceable guitar with a pedigree was stolen from Doug's guitar shop, and you recovered it here at the resort, but now the guitar has disappeared again?"

While Tony tried to explain to the deputy how the guitar had been stolen two weeks earlier, then recovered in La Crosse a day ago, the others shifted uncomfortably in their seats.

"Can we go?" asked Sarah.

"No," said the officer. "It would appear that the instrument has been stolen again, just in the past few minutes, and that makes each of you a suspect. I have no idea what sort of games you are playing here, but I need to get a statement from each of you before any of you can leave. Since there's so many of you, I've radioed in for assistance."

A second deputy was soon on the scene to help the first get statements from the guests.

"Is there anyone that we missed?" the first deputy asked as they finished their interviews. "Once we've talked with everyone, we can rap this up."

Oh crap! thought Tony. He'd forgotten about the guys from Rudy's band, the guys he couldn't find outside, the guys who told him they'd like to take the guitar out for a spin.

Chapter 36

Before anyone could inform the officers that there were two mourners unaccounted for, there came a rhythmic tapping sound from the stage.

TAP ... *TAP TAP TAP*
TAP ... *TAP TAP TAP*

The tapping grew louder.

TAP ... *TAP TAP TAP*
TAP ... *TAP TAP TAP*
TAP ... *TAP TAP TAP*
TAP ... *TAP TAP TAP*

It seemed to be coming from the back of the stage, behind the rear curtain, and echoed throughout the dance hall.

TAP ... *TAP TAP TAP*
TAP ... *TAP TAP TAP*

Everyone's attention was on the mysterious sound. Tony remembered hearing that same rhythmic tapping the first time he'd visited the boat house. Rudy had been right, the acoustics in the room were nearly perfect.

As the audience sat transfixed by the tapping, a weak, hoarse, disembodied voice began singing:

I didn't know what a kiss could mean,
'Til I met you.
I didn't know such a lovely dream
Could become true.
Then you took my breath away
Took me for a ride
In the tunnel of love...

Suddenly, two hands reached out from behind the curtains and pulled them apart, revealing a frail old man sitting on a chair, almost ghostly looking, rhythmically tapping his cane hard against the wooden stage floor. The missing Stratocaster was resting on his lap. He had a brace around his neck.

TAP *... TAP TAP TAP*
TAP *... TAP TAP TAP*

The two remaining members of Rudy's old band stepped from behind the curtains and stood at his side. They provided the backup vocals as the song continued:

In the tunnel of love...

    (Rockin' and a rollin' in the tunnel of love)
In the tunnel of love...

    (Struttin' and a strollin' in the tunnel of love)

Everyone stared at them, transfixed.

Martha stood up and began clapping in rhythm with the song. Several others joined her.

Matt grabbed the cane from Rudy's hand and continued the rhythmic tapping without missing a beat.

Tony noticed that the cord from the guitar was stretched across the stage and plugged into the amplifier. Rudy repositioned the Stratocaster, smiled, and jumped right into the song's instrumental interlude.

As Rudy and the Rockets continued singing and playing, tears flowed down Martha's cheeks. A few other cheeks were wet, as well.

When the song ended, the audience broke out in applause. Even the lawyer moved her hands politely. The deputies stood at the side of the room, not quite sure what was happening, then joined in the applause as well.

Matt took the guitar from Rudy and handed him back his cane. Rudy slowly stood up and carefully walked toward the front of the stage. When he got to the edge, he stopped and looked down.

"I think I'll stop here," he grinned. "I hear this last step is a killer."

Brian brought the chair to the front of the stage and Rudy sat down.

"I guess I've got some 'splainin' to do," he smiled, looking around the room. "And so do some of you."

Chapter 37

"We thought you were dead!" exclaimed Tony. "Not to be indelicate, but what happened?"

"What happened, is that you and your wife found me just in the nick of time. I will be forever grateful to you for that."

"How'd you end up falling off the stage in the first place?" asked Megan.

"Let me begin the story a few days before you found me. I didn't get back from Bayfield until late on Sunday. That's cause I decided to spend an extra day up there with these two knuckleheads."

He nodded to Matt and Brian, who were still with him on the stage.

"You two might as well grab a seat and listen with the others. This might take awhile."

They left the stage and pulled up chairs behind the others, near the back of the room.

"When I got up on Monday morning," Rudy began, "I went into the kitchen, same as always, to prepare my usual smoothie. I was pleased to find that someone had left me a full bag of greens in the refrigerator. I figured Sarah had picked them for me. She was pretty good at doing little things like that to help me out.

"But before I could get started, Tony pulled up to tell me about the guitar being stolen and offered to take me out for breakfast, so I put the greens back in the fridge and we went looking for the guitar.

"The next morning, I popped a couple slices of bread in the toaster, then went out to my garden and picked some raspberries. I thought I smelled the toast burning and hurried inside. I was relieved that there wasn't any smoke coming from the toaster, but the toast was blacker than I liked. Normally I'd have tossed it in the trash, but they were my last two slices of bread so I simply slathered them with butter and jam. Then I tossed the raspberries into the blender along with the mixed greens and added some pineapple juice that'd been in the fridge.

"After breakfast, I began to feel a bit queasy. I wondered if the juice had gone bad. I went into the Great Hall and sat down in my favorite, overstuffed chair. The busier-than-usual weekend and events of the previous day had obviously worn me out. I felt exhausted, a bit dizzy and my chest hurt, which concerned me.

"As I sat there, I felt worse. Everything I looked at seemed to have a yellow aura around it. I needed to calm down my heart, so I settled into the chair and closed my eyes.

"After what seemed like only a few minutes, I woke up because I thought I smelled smoke again. I knew I hadn't left any bread in the toaster because I'd just eaten the last two slices, burned as they were. Then I heard a voice. A woman's voice that I didn't recognize at the time. Very distinct, high pitched. Reminded me of Betty Boop."

He stared at Cassidy.

"It seemed like the voice was coming from down the hall. I listened closely without moving a muscle. To be honest, I wasn't so sure that my muscles would move even if I tried.

"I heard the voice say. 'It worked. He's gone.' Apparently the woman believed that she'd poisoned me and was reporting in with the good news."

Thomas suddenly stood up. He glanced back and forth between Rudy and the deputies.

"She wasn't calling me," he asserted, panicking. "I'm sorry I stole your guitar. My buddy said I should take it and he'd sell it and we'd split the money. But I didn't have anything to do with trying to kill you."

"Glad to hear that. Any ideas who you think it was?"

"It must have been Sarah. She's the one who recruited me for this stupid role."

Sarah looked at him, horrified.

"It wasn't Sarah," said Rudy before the young woman could defend herself. "I know her voice. And I trust her. But I'm none too happy with you for stealing my guitar. Allow me to continue."

Thomas sat down, wishing he'd kept his mouth shut.

"Sarah," Rudy said, looking directly at the young woman. "What did Thomas mean when he said you recruited him for this role?"

"I didn't actually recruit him. I barely knew him before this all began. I just agreed with the casting director that Thomas seemed like he'd be good in the role."

"And what role was that?"

"We were cast to be your friends. We're both actors

from Chicago. We were hired to charm our way into your life and convince you to sell your resort to Apex Land Development."

"They hired us for six months," added Thomas. "They provided us with a small weekly stipend and promised that we'd receive a bonus of fifty-thousand dollars each if, by the end of our six-month contract, you had agreed to sell to Apex."

"There was never any mention of you including us in your will," Sarah said," but I do think that was awfully nice of you."

"Sarah, Sarah, Sarah," Rudy said, delicately shaking his head. "I never wrote that will. It was a forgery, apparently planted by Apex so they'd get the Foxglove property, free and clear. The bonus they promised you, that would come from my estate."

He paused and did some quick calculating in his head.

"It's been six months this week since you showed up at my door with your hard-luck story."

"Tell me about it," grumbled Thomas. "It was obvious that you weren't going to sell to Apex and I wasn't going to get my bonus. I deserved some sort of reward for having had to put up with Sarah in that dinky little cabin you stuck us in. I can see why she's single."

Sarah gave the pitiful young man a sad look, then looked to Rudy.

"It was just supposed to be a fun little improv assignment with a big payout at the end," she explained. "But as I got to know you, as we became friends, I realized that you took us in because you're a truly nice person who wanted nothing more than to help us. I'm sorry that we deceived you. I didn't have anything to do with trying to kill you."

"Neither did I," added Thomas, crossing himself. "Scout's honor."

Chapter 38

"I guess that leaves us with who did try to kill me," said Rudy.

He shifted in his chair. Obviously he was still in some pain from the injuries sustained in his fall.

"Where was I?"

"You told us that you heard some woman telling someone that something had worked and someone was gone and you figured that that someone was you and the woman apparently thought she had poisoned you," summarized Tony.

"Well, that clears things up, doesn't it," Rudy laughed. He paused, took a deep breath, then continued his story.

"I didn't hear any other voices, so I figured she was talking on her phone. A few moments later, I heard the sound of a door opening at the end of the hall. I recognized it because that door sticks and makes a squeaking sound when it's opened, and it's hard to pull closed. It's the tunnel door that leads down to the boat house.

"I decided I needed to investigate. I could barely keep my balance when I stood up, but with the aid of my trusty cane I made it to the end of the hallway. The door to the tunnel was partially open, a still smouldering cigarette butt dropped at the entrance, which pissed me off because it wouldn't take much for an old log building like the lodge to go up in flames. I stomped it out with my cane, then carefully made my way into the tunnel.

"I couldn't hear any sounds ahead of me, so I wasn't sure if this was the way she had escaped or if the open door and cigarette butt were there for misdirection. By the way," he added as an aside, "mystery writers do that too often."

"By the time I made my way down to the boat house, I was completely exhausted. My heart was pumping like it wanted to jump out of my chest. Everything was spinning and that yellow aura in my vision had gotten worse. Stepping into the light after being in the dark tunnel didn't help.

"I remembered that I had some bottles of water stashed along the side of the stage, so I gathered all my strength and made my way up here into the dance hall. It was dark at the top of the stairs behind the curtain. I didn't hear or see anyone.

"I pushed my way through the curtain and headed across the stage to get a bottle of water. All of a sudden my cane was jerked out from under me and I fell forward. I didn't know who had attacked me or why.

"In fact, I didn't know who had attacked me until a few minutes ago, while I was backstage, and I heard that Betty Boop voice and peeked through the curtain to see who it was."

He glared at Cassidy as he said: "I realized that you'd put the foxglove in my greens, tripped me on the stage and left me to die."

"It wasn't my idea," said Cassidy, jumping up. She pointed at the lawyer. "She made me do it. It was all her idea. She's the one I called to report that you were dead. You can check her phone."

The matter-of-fact confession coming from such a child-like voice was chilling.

"When I heard you following me down the tunnel, I panicked. I had just called in to report that you were dead and there was no way I was going to call her back and say, 'Whoops! Got it wrong.' I hurried up to the stage and hid behind the curtain, trying to decide what to do. That's when I noticed a long pole with a hook on the end. When you stumbled out onto the stage I grabbed it and used it to pull your cane out from under you."

She paused for a breath.

"When I walked over to where you lay and saw the blood, I was sure that this time you were dead for real. I'd completed my assignment, so I left and didn't look back."

"You left me to die," said the old man.

The deputies came forward and removed Cassidy and the lawyer from the room, but instructed the others to remain where they were.

After a long silence, Rudy, still sitting in the chair, began to cough and motioned for a bottle of water. Martha jumped up, grabbed one, opened it, handed it to him, then sat back down.

After a long, slow drink he said: "I guess this is what it's like to grow old and have to depend on your children to take care of you."

Several folks in the room laughed.

"It was in the hospital that my life took a major turn," he said. "As you've heard, Martha had suspected that I might be her father and she showed me the results of the paternity test.

"I never had any idea that Annie had had a baby, that I had a daughter. I was both shocked and thrilled. I'd always believed that Rudolf James Rogers was the last name on my family tree. Suddenly I realized that wasn't true. Martha gave me a reason to live."

Several folks glanced at Martha and nodded their support. Megan gave her a thumbs up.

"Martha," asked Megan, "why did you tell us that Rudy had died? I'm thrilled to see that he is alive, but I have to admit, I feel a bit deceived."

"That was my fault," said the old man. "Someone tried to kill me but there was no evidence. As some of you know, I have always idolized Hercule Poirot. Suddenly I had a murder to solve—my own—and I couldn't resist putting my little gray cells into action. Of course, to do that, I needed to be dead."

"In my defense," said Martha, "I never specifically said that he had died. As I recall, when I phoned you from the hospital I told you that Rudy 'had left the building.' I let you believe I was being cute and that he had passed away."

"So, basically, you kidnapped him and hid him in a little cabin the woods," quipped Tony. "Reminds me of a Stephen King story."

"No. No," said Rudy. "Wrong author. I was voluntarily released into her care. The doctor knew that she'd cared for her mother for several years and trusted that she could assist me in my recovery. It was either that or I'd get transferred to a nursing home for rehabilitation."

"If you thought someone tried to murder you, why didn't you go to the police?" asked Tony.

"With what evidence? By the time you found me, there were only traces of digitalis left in my blood and since I was taking digitalis for my heart condition that didn't raise any red flags. Martha told me that the blender I used to make the smoothie had been washed clean. I needed to figure out a way for the guilty parties to reveal themselves. That's when I came up with the idea for today's event, which worked out even better than I'd expected."

"You may recall," said Martha, "that we never once called this gathering a funeral or memorial. We invited you to a 'celebration of Rudy's life,' which is absolutely true."

"I'm sorry to have deceived you," said Rudy. "Like some of you in this room, I guess I'm guilty of making believe I was something I was not."

Rudy turned to Sarah. "I have a question for you. Who hired the two of you to befriend me?"

"We got the job through the casting agency and that's who paid us our stipends. But at the murder mystery dinner, I discovered that the person who'd actually hired us was the man who came to that event as Sonny.

"While he and I were talking on the front porch, I'd commented to him how beautiful the view was from there and he said to just imagine what it'll be like from the balconies of the twenty-four luxury condos he was planning to build here, next to his golf course. That's when I discovered he was the president of Apex Land

Development. He complimented me on doing a great job in my role and assured me that it wouldn't be much longer before I got my bonus. I assumed that meant that he'd come to an agreement with you to sell him the resort."

"I've never met the man," Rudy said. "The proposals to buy the resort had come from Apex's legal counsel. When I learned that she was the same person named as executor of my estate, I realized that the wills had been switched."

"Does that mean that the will we signed is real?" asked Sarah.

"It does, but that's immaterial since I'm alive. Which reminds me, would the representatives from the library, homeless shelter and history museum please contact me in the next day or two to schedule a meeting with Martha and me. We need to begin the process of drafting new documents that will better support the mission and realities of your organizations ... and my heir."

Martha stood up. "Thank you everyone," she said, "for coming here to help celebrate the life of Rudy Rogers, your friend and my father."

As the people began leaving, the deputy told Sarah and Thomas that the sheriff's department would be contacting them and not to leave the state.

When Megan, Tony, Martha and Rudy were the only people left in the boat house, Megan said, "I have one more question. For Martha. Were the ashes that you cast over the railing from your fireplace? If so, it was a very convincing performance."

"It was no performance," said Martha. "Those were the remains of my mother, Annie. I realized that I had finally found the perfect place and time to scatter her ashes. And the perfect people to share the moment with me."

She looked at Rudy.

"While the rest of you were up on the deck," he explained, "I was below you in the boat house, scattering some of Annie's ashes at the same time."

Tony stepped up on the stage and pushed the button on the cassette player. "Anyone want to dance?"

• • • • •

Cassidy and her boss were charged with attempted murder.

Apex Development and its president were under investigation for their involvement and for their attempt to illegally seize the Foxglove Resort property.

Thomas and his pony-tailed friend were charged with robbery and attempting to sell stolen goods.

Rudy and Martha set up a trust that would allow them to support the library and homeless shelter and also build a long-term plan for the eventual development of Foxglove Resort as a living history museum.

One of the first steps toward that end was to renovate the three remaining cabins. Two of them would be used for vacation rentals, the same as they were originally designed.

The third cabin was reserved as the residence for a live-in caretaker who could look after the yards and gardens. They hoped to offer that job to Sarah.

At the end of the summer, on Labor Day weekend, another celebration was held in the boat house at Foxglove Resort. This time it was a social event and everyone was welcome. Signs were posted around town inviting the community to a free reunion concert in the boat house dance hall featuring Rudy and the Rockets.

As the band played, Megan shared a table with Martha, imagining themselves back in 1962 watching the band for the first time and having school-girl crushes on the musicians.

Rudy had healed well from his fall. His voice was nearly back in form and the sounds he coaxed from his Stratocaster were as exciting as ever.

Brian was on bass, the same as always, but Matt had switched over to drums, which meant they had a guest rhythm guitar player for that special event.

Proudly strumming one of Rudy's other vintage guitars, beaming from ear to ear, was some guy they picked up off the streets.

Tony.

To Kevin
Love, Rudy Rogers
Rudy and
the Rockets

TUNNEL OF LOVE

I didn't know what a kiss could mean,
'til I met you.
I didn't know such a lovely dream
Could become true
Then you took my breath away,
Took me for a ride!
In the tunnel of love....
  (rockin' & a rollin' in the tunnel of love)
  (struttin' and a strollin' in the tunnel of love)

One night one moment shared,
Are you really true?
Twists and turns but never scared,
I'm in love with you.
Then you stole my heart away,
Took me for a ride!
In the tunnel of love....
  (splishin' & a splashin' in the tunnel of love)
  (movin' and a groovin' in the tunnel of love)
In the tunnel of love....
  (dancin' & a prancin' in the tunnel of love)
  (twistin' and a turnin' in the tunnel of love)

Written Aug. 5, 1962
by Rudy Rogers, at Foxglove Resort

Listen to "Tunnel of Love" by Rudy and the Rockets

Books by David L. Tank

Blackbird Cabin Cozy Mystery Series
- The Secret of Blackbird Cabin
- The Secrets of Foxglove Lodge

Secret Santa Middle-Grade Time-Travel Adventure Series
- The Mystery of the Stereoscope
- The Mystery of the Magic Watch
- The Mystery of the Lost Guitar
- The Mystery of the Moving Picture

Postcards from the Past Series
- Then and Now Pictures of Menomonie, Wisconsin
- Then and Now Pictures of Dunn County, Wisconsin
- Then and Now Pictures of Eau Claire, Wisconsin
- Then and Now Pictures of Chippewa Falls, Wisconsin
- Then and Now Pictures of Wisconsin's Northwoods

3D Photography
- Wisconsin Wildflowers in 3D
- The Magic of 3D Photography

Children's Picture Books
- Half Pint
- The Lumberjack and the Eagle

Other
- Uncle Eggbert's Egg Book (cook book)
- River of Hope (memoir)